**'There are so n...
Ellie, which a...
elusive and rea...**

'I want to find out all about you,' Ben continued, 'to discover a clue to this intense relationship, for I'm pretty sure...' His gaze was now so dominating she had no power to look elsewhere, no power to move aside as his hand came up to brush a strand of hair from her forehead, no power to hide the shiver as his fingers lingered against her cheek.

'What I can't work out, Ellie, is why, when you have so many adverse feelings, you are here in the first place.'

She sat up, dislodging his hand. Impossible to give an answer since there was none. If she were to tell the truth she would be humiliated, and if she lied... She was as obsessed with Ben Congreve as she had ever been. And for that she despised herself.

Alexandra Scott was born in Scotland and lived there until she met her husband, who was serving in the British Army, and there followed twenty-five years of travel in the Far East and Western Europe. They then settled in North Yorkshire and, encouraged by her husband, she began writing romantic novels. Her other interests include gardening and embroidery, and she enjoys the company of her family.

Recent titles by the same author:

A RECKLESS AFFAIR

CHARLIE'S DAD

BY
ALEXANDRA SCOTT

MILLS & BOON®

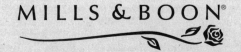

*First published in Great Britain 1998
Harlequin Mills & Boon Limited,
Eton House, 18-24 Paradise Road, Richmond, Surrey TW9 1SR*

© Alexandra Scott 1998

ISBN 0 263 80828 9

*Set in Times Roman 10½ on 12 pt.
02-9806-51898 C1*

*Printed and bound in Great Britain
by Mackays of Chatham PLC, Chatham*

CHAPTER ONE

'YOU'RE on your way, Ellie Osborne. The past is dead.'

That was the final shibboleth, the only part of her dream which remained in her mind as she struggled to raise her eyelids, which felt as if they had been coated with Superglue. Then, when she at last succeeded, she gasped at the sight of the clock by her bedside.

'A-a-ah!' The sigh became a groan as she realised she ought by this time to be up and dressed, not indulging herself in this fashion. It was simply that she was bone-weary after so much travelling. Imperceptibly her eyes were drifting again, her brain flirting with all the intense activity involved since her departure from Heathrow less than a week ago. Making excuses.

Not that it had been unsuccessful, she mused in dreamy satisfaction. Far from it. In fact, the contract signed yesterday in Hong Kong would be the kick-start she needed for expansion, what she had hoped for—and dreaded—over the years. Now all was within her grasp and the future beckoned.

Not that it had been easy. Amusing to recall her beginnings, five, six years ago, when she had set up her machine on the kitchen table and sold her knitted garments at a tiny profit in London's street markets.

She gave another sighing yawn. No, those early customers had no idea how lucky they had been to be offered IGRAINE originals for little more than peanuts. Not that the name or the logo had been registered then.

5

Those had come later, along with the chic silk labels and the media coverage led by that very first television interview in Hong Kong. Which in turn had led to her present visit to Singapore instead of heading immediately back to London.

A tap at the door made her look up, and she smiled as Jenny came into the bedroom carrying a cup of tea which Ellie took, sipping gratefully. 'Delicious. I'm lying here feeling guilty. I just hope I'm not holding things up, Jenny.'

'You must have been tired. I looked in half an hour ago, but you were so peaceful I decided to leave you till the last possible moment.'

'Lazy, rather. But this—' she drained the cup and put it on the bedside table '—was exactly what I needed to wake me up. I was just thinking of that interview you did when we first met in Hong Kong.' She swung long, slender legs over the side of the bed. 'You're sure I'm not holding things up?'

'No, you have lots of time. It will be an hour before the dinner guests arrive.' Jenny crossed the room, twitched one of the net curtains, then swung round to raise an eyebrow at her visitor. 'But I'm hoping, with luck, you'll emerge before then. Robert is so impatient to meet you.'

'And I'm dying to meet him too.' With firm determination she got to her feet and stretched. 'So, I have time to shower and…' She ran fingers through the mass of dark auburn hair which had escaped from its pins. 'Time for a shampoo as well, do you think?'

'If you hurry. You'll find a drier in your bathroom.'

'Would you believe, I haven't washed it since I left

home? I meant to be up in time this morning, but my call was late and it was a mad rush to get to the airport.'

'I'll leave you then.' Jenny, small-boned and exquisite in the understated way of elegant Chinese women, reached the door, pausing with her hand on the knob. 'What were you saying about that first television interview?'

Ellie crossed to the dressing table and began to rummage in her toilet bag. 'Just thinking about it.' Smiling, she unscrewed a jar, dipped a finger into the moisturiser, transferred the pale blob to her skin. 'I was lying, half dreaming, and that was what came into my mind the instant you tapped on the door. You've no idea how many times I've blessed you for that.'

'But it was simply chance. We were short of an item for the programme we were putting out live—about people who were coming from overseas and using the local labour force—and someone, I think it was Johnny Teck, mentioned your name. Actually, I was grateful to you for agreeing to come on at such short notice.'

Ellie, making for the bathroom, shook her head. 'Never refuse the offer of free publicity—one of the first rules of running your own business. Just a mention on TV or radio can mean the difference between success and failure. Oh—' Just before disappearing, she remembered. 'Would you mind if I made a quick call to Charlie? I usually try to ring home about now.'

'You don't have to ask.' Jenny waved a slender hand towards the telephone on a side-table. 'I still can't understand why Charlie and I have never met. Oh, and by the way, honey…' Again, Jenny paused. 'One of our guests this evening is Jonas Parnell, the American writer. I'm sure, like me, you've read every one of his bestsellers. I'm always so impatient for the next one to come out. His father is a friend of Robert's.' And with that the door finally closed.

'Jonas Parnell?' As Ellie held her face up into the stream of warm water, began to rub some flowery unguent into her hair, she murmured the name. Vaguely it rang a bell, but since she had little time for reading, apart from balance sheets... On the other hand, there had been that late-night movie a few weekends back—a hectic, fast-paced murder mystery... Jonas Parnell...that name forced itself into her mind. At the time, anxious for bed, she had been half irritated by its compulsion—certainly she had found it exciting enough to keep her glued to the screen till long past her normal bedtime, when sleep was what she needed most.

Rubbing her hair with a soft towel, she stepped from the shower, crossed the bedroom and reached for the telephone. She began to dial her home number and a moment later she spoke. 'Charlie, darling.' Her voice, always soft and melodious, grew still more tender. 'You wouldn't believe how much I'm missing you.'

'Not too bad.' Surveying her reflection with a critical eye, Ellie turned this way and that before giving a tiny smile of satisfaction. Evening affairs hardly figured in her diary these days, and she had almost fallen out of the habit of making the effort. And now, she was forced to conclude with what was very nearly a grin, that seemed a pity. A successful effort did wonders for one's ego, quite regardless of any impression it made on others.

Besides, she owed it to Jenny to put her best foot forward. It would be humiliating if she, an up-and-coming designer, were to disappoint her hostess. To say nothing of Robert Van Tieg, whom she would for the first time be meeting.

Much of their story she already knew—how Jenny, very soon after their first encounter, had moved in with the wealthy entrepreneur. Theirs was a perfectly open relationship, and when Ellie had once hinted that it might lead to marriage, Jenny had immediately jumped on such a suggestion, insisting the present arrangement suited them admirably.

'You see,' she had explained, 'Robert has been married twice, both times unsuccessfully, and I had never planned any kind of long-term relationship. Not until I met Robert, that is, then I instantly changed my mind. That I'm still with him is rather against my own principles.' Here she had grinned, slightly embarrassed. 'But you see, I just love the guy. Can you understand?'

'Yes.' Ellie had disregarded the ache in her chest. 'Of course I can.' Who better to understand than Ellie Osborne?

'And besides,' Jenny had gone on swiftly, 'I have my career, he has his business interests. We each allow the other complete freedom, never question the need for this or that, and the funny thing is, between us there is complete trust. Even though I know he is meeting so many fascinating women—many of whom would be more than willing to join him in a fling—doubts about his fidelity never enter my mind.'

Jenny *was* lucky. Making final adjustments to her make-up, Ellie reflected on her friend's good fortune with not the least trace of jealousy. Rich, beautiful, with one of the world's most successful businessmen in love with her, and a television career going strong on both sides of the Pacific, who could deny that fortune had smiled on Jenny Seow? What was still more astonishing was that she was so unspoiled, so unaffected by the huge sums she earned through TV shows syndicated world-wide.

Satisfied at last, Ellie stepped back from the mirror, her attention now wholly focused on her reflection, relieved to confirm it would satisfy the most critical eye. And all credit for that to Jean Muir. What had at the time seemed like quite unjustified extravagance, mark-down price notwithstanding, now began to look like a serious long-term investment. All those sleepless nights spent worrying over such unprecedented self-indulgence…she gave a tiny giggle. A sheer waste of effort.

It was undeniable that the overall appearance was timeless and elegant. Quite seriously she could see herself wearing the same outfit twenty years from now: wide trousers in damson scribbled all over with cream, the floaty material giving occasional glimpses of long legs, and a tunic top, matching but plain, neckline and cuffs edged with cream braid. It was so stunning she couldn't imagine why she didn't wear it more often, and certainly for a smart supper party here in Singapore it was perfect.

After some consideration, she left her hair loose, abandoning her more usual French pleat for the pleasure of it moving about her face like sensuous silk. Make-up was understated, lips outlined with a soft subtle plum, and eyes—well, those she had always considered the best features in an unremarkable face, and she had summoned all her skill to emphasise the clear translucent grey, just that rim of black round the irises causing the whites to gleam. A last unnecessary touch of the wand to already sooty lashes, a blast of perfume and she was ready. Automatically her hand reached out for the solitaire diamond which she slid alongside the plain gold band on her left hand.

He was nothing like she had imagined. Standing with other guests on the balcony while Robert pointed out some focal points of the city, Ellie found it difficult to avoid comparisons. Jenny, so petite, so slender and striking, and Robert… Well, handsome he was not—short, thickset, and with the powerful shoulders of a prize fighter—although with his air of power and wealth it wasn't difficult to see how he might attract women.

Impeccable manners and dress—these she had expected—but the heavy features, the shrewd eyes partly concealed behind tinted glasses…no, he was not at all the kind of man she had been looking forward to meeting. There was, she knew, a twelve-year age difference, but he looked a good twenty years older than Jenny. However, in spite of conflicting impressions, she found herself warming to him, enjoying a sense of humour which was dry and sardonic, even slightly self-deprecating. That was something of a shock; high-flying businessmen did not, at least in her experience, take life so lightly.

Then came a diversion. Jenny was ushering a new arrival through the French windows and onto the balcony and was engaged in animated conversation. Ellie caught the deep cadence of a laugh which brought her head jerking up in perplexed alarm, her wide eyes staring, but all she could discern was that the newcomer was male, dressed in a tropical suit in dark grey, a pinkish shirt, and that Jenny was smiling up at him, her face glowing with delight.

Jenny was now trying to attract Robert's attention and he excused himself, making his way across the expanse of pale-coloured marble towards the window. There was a short silence as his guests watched, a silence broken by Pete, a rangy Australian who had been introduced as a business acquaintance.

'Robert's quite a personality, isn't he?'

Ellie's eyes were still on the group by the window, slightly aggrieved that the newcomer—the American writer, she supposed—was still hidden by some trailing exotic plants. Reluctantly she dragged herself back to see Pete nod in the direction of his young pretty wife.

'Babs has never met him before tonight. What did you think of him, honey?'

'Robert's everything you said, but I guess he'll take a bit of getting to know.'

'Like his taste in women, though.' Raising his glass, Pete drank deeply, as if underlining his approval of Jenny.

Ellie exchanged an amused glance with Babs, who shrugged philosophically and immediately changed the subject. 'You've come from England on business, Ellie?'

Ellie leaned an arm against the wrought-iron balustrade, idly watching the lights of a ship sailing into the harbour. 'Yes, I have my own small fashion company—knitted garments. I've been finalising details with some of the Hong Kong companies who make up my designs. I'm on my way home now, but broke my journey to visit Jenny and Robert.'

'Using wool from Oz, I hope?' Pete's interest was solely commercial.

'Take no notice of him, Ellie. Just because his Dad's in sheep…'

'Well, I'm sorry about that.' Turning from the view with a smile, Ellie leaned against the balcony, arms extended, face raised to the balmy evening air. 'But we pride ourselves on using only the best English wools, specially blended for us, occasionally with the addition of silk. But if ever I feel the need to use Australian wools I'll remember your father. In fact, I have connections with Australia myself, and I…'

The words dried on her lips as Jenny, Robert and their guest moved against the window behind them, the light from the room illuminating the two faces she knew but leaving the other irritatingly half hidden, mysterious. He was well above average height, the new man, and dark. His head was bent towards his hostess, and the casual, easy way he supported himself, with one arm crooked against a pillar…there was something about him, something which made her catch her breath, made her aware of an icy drip of water the length of her spine…

'You were saying, Ellie…' Babs prompted.

'I…' For a second she stared at the young woman, unable to recall the drift of the conversation. Her heart was beating loudly against her ribs… 'Ah, yes, what was I saying, Babs? About wools, wasn't it? England has such a wide range of fleeces that it seems more sensible,' she gabbled. 'After all, I doubt that you drink much English wine.'

Oblivious of the puzzled expression which her remark elicited she heard her voice prattle on for a few more seconds, but her mind was engaged with a quite different subject.

Deliberately she kept her attention away from the

group she found so inexplicably disturbing, smiling vaguely at her companions, determined to concentrate, to dismiss idle speculation from her mind. But it was such a weird feeling, frightening, as if things long past were threatening to catch up with her, events she would prefer to keep buried...

'Ellie, I told you we were expecting Jonas Parnell, now I'd like you to meet him.'

Ellie turned. Her intense grey eyes, shadowy with apprehension swept over Jenny and Robert, unwillingly but inevitably drawn to the man who loomed over them all. Jenny's tinkling laugh rang out.

'Only his name isn't Jonas Parnell, it's Ben Congreve. Ben, this is a dear friend, Ellie Osborne.'

It was all automatic then. Ellie held out her hand, hoping the smile she fixed on her face would conceal her shock, and it was a great help that she saw not the faintest sign of recognition in his eyes. Admiration, perhaps—she thought she could discern a flicker of that—and interest, curiosity. But nothing more. So, it was safe to smile, to relax, or at least to make an effort in that direction. Otherwise she had no idea how she would deal with the hours of torment which lay ahead.

She stood there, taking little part in the conversation washing about her, trying desperately to deal with the raging assault of emotions. For who could have forecast the crossing of their paths like this after so many fraught years? Long, long after she had felt any need—after all, it was a lifetime since she had given up all expectation. Years during which hope had slowly and, oh, dear God, how painfully...died.

'You know Singapore well, Ellie?' Ben Congreve, sitting to her right, waited till she had finished her chat with Pete before demanding her attention, forcing her to look at him so he could check. Mmm. He felt a moment of sheer pleasure as the clear grey eyes flicked him a glance. A slightly nervous glance, he decided, though it was inconceivable such a self-possessed and seemingly successful woman should be either shy or nervous. He had never, he thought in a spirit of self-mockery, seen such eyes... And set in that face... So serene, so astonishingly...well, it was more than merely beautiful—fascinating, rather, with those high cheekbones, that exciting mouth, such a rippling cascade of titian hair.

He caught at himself, smiling inwardly at such an uncharacteristic response, but found he was unwilling to deny himself the pleasure of analysis. Perfect skin too. A bloom like a peach—and that was scarcely original. And for a writer too.

'Not well.' Such an effort to keep her voice so calm and even, but no one, she thought, no one could possibly guess that her heart was agitating wildly against her ribs, that her palms were so moist they threatened her grip on her fork. 'I've been here several times but always for very short spells so I can't claim to know it.'

Now she could return her attention to her plate, spoon some of the delicious terrine into her mouth. 'You?' Another glance in his direction confirmed what she feared, that he was still focused on her, bringing a wave of unwelcome heat to her body.

His faint smile told her he had noticed, but he had the grace to look away, to apply himself to the food on his plate and at the same time deal with her question. 'The same. I don't know it well, but since the book I'm writing has a scene set here I thought I'd come and do some research before getting down to the grind of actual writ-

ing. All writers are like that, you know—any excuse to
avoid the tyranny of the word processor.'

'Mmm. So I've heard. But I thought it was invented
to make life easier for you.'

'That's the theory.' He slanted another glance towards
her; he was surprising himself with his desire to divert
and amuse this woman. 'But I'm wholly unconvinced. I
must be honest and admit that writing is a love-hate
affair, almost a voluntary slavery. There are times when
I want to be rid of the whole demanding business, and
then…as soon as I have finished what I had decided was
to be my last…something jogs the brain. One or two
ideas which have been drifting loose seem determined
to come together and so, before I can do a thing about
it, I'm off. Back to the treadmill.'

'Ben!' Jenny was mildly reproving. 'You make it
sound as if you have to labour over every word, and yet
your prose…each word you write…flows so effortlessly
onto the page.'

'Ah…' He shook his head in self-mocking derision.
'That is where the genius comes in.'

There was a wave of laughter round the table before
the argument was taken up at a more individual level,
which gave him the opportunity to turn again to the
woman by his side. 'And now you know all about me,
it's my turn to hear about you.'

She had little choice but to turn and look at him, lips
curving into a smile that was more than a little reluctant.
He was so very easy to look at, but that had always been
so. Tall, good-looking, arresting without being conven-
tionally handsome, dark silky hair… Even now she
could feel a throb at the thought of twisting it through
her fingers. Shorter now, of course, and the buccaneering

look had gone, along with the beard. And those slender well-marked eyebrows, which would arch upwards when he was waiting for an answer…as he was now.

'But there isn't a great deal to tell.' By any standard of veracity that was an outright lie. Her life, though reasonably conventional on the surface, hid a dark and wounded side which she refused to discuss, especially with a mystery writer, and certainly not with…

But he was obviously waiting for elucidation, so in a move which was habitual, defensive—one she found herself using when she felt particularly vulnerable—she raised her left hand to brush a strand of hair from her cheek, displaying her rings before allowing her hand to drop.

'I don't know if Robert mentioned it, but I have my own small fashion company—mainly knitwear, until now mostly made in the UK, but an increasing number are now produced in Hong Kong. I was there for several days and Jenny invited me here for a break before going home. It's a plan which has been thwarted several times in the last two years—'

'And I'm delighted you were able to make it at last.' From the other side of the table Jenny interrupted, then there was a slight hiatus as plates were cleared, fresh dishes brought by the unobtrusive maids.

And Ellie, as she listened half-heartedly to what Pete, on her other side was trying to explain, wished with all her heart she had flown back to Heathrow. By this time she would have been with Charlie. All the reawakening heartbreak would have been avoided. Earlier this evening she had been right to decide this was not her milieu, that she was out of touch with this kind of socialising.

She experienced a sensation of despair as she allowed

her attention to drift round the sophisticated room: light net curtains billowing in a faint breeze, modern paintings set against cream walls, a green marble dining table. Green marble! And with the most intricate veining in gold. Food arranged with precise artistry on black plates, each a study…

A sudden flash of recollection brought a smile to her lips. She was thinking of the pot of stew she so frequently put on the table—the scrubbed kitchen table—the homely loaf of bread which she might have made during a therapeutic break but which was inevitably lopsided and collapsing, though still ideal for mopping up gravy. The bowl of hastily put together salad leaves…

Light years from this arrangement of skewered seafood surrounded by tiny mounds of saffron rice and compositions—the word was not too extravagant—of vegetables she didn't begin to recognise. It was almost too artistic to eat, something her own meals never were, but…the contrast of colours was inspired. She had an instant vision of a shift sweater, basic black like the plate but with swirls of gamboge, a touch of shrimp-pink and that particular green… If only her brain could retain the colours. Fingers twitching, she longed for her sketchpad and paintbrush…

'Aren't you going to eat?' The gentle query took her head round to look at him, eyebrows arching quizzically, mouth curving in sheer pleasure before she remembered to control them.

'Oh, yes.' A moment's breathless glowing enthusiasm, then searing pain as she recognised that particular expression, the way his eyes moved slowly over her features before coming to rest, with quite unmistakable meaning, on her mouth. 'Of course.'

Soberly, determined to ignore the knot of misery in her chest she switched her focus back to her plate, picked up her fork. 'It is all so…so beautiful.' Delicately she detached a scallop, raised it to her mouth. 'Don't you agree?' What was intended to be a quick casual glance in his direction was arrested, caught and held.

'Yes.' The reply came slow and deliberate, making it obvious that the food was not on his mind. 'Oh, yes, I agree.'

Beautiful. Even when he turned to exchange a few words with his partner on the other side, it was her face which occupied his mind. Such white teeth, not perfect exactly, with a slight overlapping of the front two, a generous, giving mouth which he would have liked to feel against his, and when she smiled… It occurred to him she didn't do that often enough, but when she did her whole face lit up. She had an inner glow which intrigued, wakening his interest, a stirring of excitement which had long been absent from his life, except…

As he conversed his lips moved automatically. Except…

Except that he was picking up discouraging signals. He had been fully aware of that informative gesture of her left hand but… But, he was not going to allow the possibility of a husband in the background to deter him from finding out more about this intriguing woman.

Dead on her feet or not, Ellie found sleep elusive that first night in the Van Tieg apartment. Nothing to do with the heat of the sultry tropical night; that was held at bay by efficient air-conditioning. Nothing to do with that and everything to do with the man she had long ago dismissed from her consciousness. But if she had been as efficient in that as she believed, why was he now causing her so much emotional havoc?

Ellie groaned, pushed a hand through the heavy fall of hair and thrust her face deeper into the pillow. If only sleep would come. She was desperate for the chance to forget Ben Congreve for a few hours. In the morning, she knew from experience, things would look entirely more reasonable. For one thing there was no need for her ever to meet up with him again. Tomorrow would be her last day in Singapore. After that she would be flying back to her own life, to Charlie. Ah, yes, Charlie, on whom the whole sorry saga hinged.

And then, without any decision on her part, without volition or even co-operation, her mind was clicking with the memories which she had tried to hold at bay, sweeping her back through the years to the time when she had first known Ben Congreve. That halcyon, magical time... The knowledge that the whole exercise was mere self-indulgence had no power to stop her.

Twenty years old with the world before her. That had been her father's smug description on the day she had been awarded her degree at Sydney University. And as a reward he had handed her a cheque to subsidise her declared longing to travel for a few months before settling down to a career in fashion.

'Or teaching perhaps?' Sir William had distrusted his daughter's ambition to try her luck in the rag trade. His leaning was towards a more conventional and, as he thought, a more secure career.

'Yes.' Helen, as she had been known then, had long ago found it made life much easier to go along with her parents' suggestions, or at least to go through the motions. 'If there are no openings in the fashion world, I promise you, I'll try teaching.'

'Well, if you make for London, I'm sure you'll find plenty of openings. Your mother and I are very proud of you—a year younger than most of your class and carrying off the top awards. The cheque is to show how much.'

'You're very generous, Dad.' Reaching up, she kissed his cheek. 'And you're sure you don't mind me going off on my own for a few years?'

'We'll miss you, of course. But you've lost a lot of your childhood through your mother's illness and we both want to make up to you for that.'

'Dad, you can't help that—and certainly Mother didn't ask to be struck down with multiple sclerosis. You don't have to make up to me.'

'Nevertheless, it's what we decided. You know we would both like to go back to the old country, but since the climate here suits your mother so much more... Anyway, I ought to tell you, I'm thinking of retiring from the Diplomatic Corps. I've been approached by a major Japanese company to take over a management position here in Sydney, and I'm tempted for your mother's sake...'

'Dad, you dark horse. I'm the one who ought to be rewarding you, not the other way round.'

'No.' He grinned. 'All I ask is that you write often to your mother. You know how she has missed England. Just keep the letters and postcards coming.'

'I promise. Only...you won't mind too much if I make my way to Europe via the Caribbean, will you? Some of the diving club are planning an excavation of an old

Spanish galleon that's been discovered off the Windwards, and they've asked me to go along.'

'We-ell, I suppose you've made up your mind about that already. So…all I ask is that you'll be careful. I don't want your mother to be worried—you know the effect it can have on her condition if she's anxious, especially if she's anxious about her only child.'

'I promise.' Again she stood on tiptoe to drop a kiss on his cheek. 'I promise I'll be very careful. I'm not into risk-taking and I'll write as often as I can.'

And that was how, a week after her twenty-first birthday she came to touch down in the Windwards, one of three girls in a group of seven from Sydney, joining several teams from American Universities excavating the seventeenth-century schooner which had foundered in a storm. And that was how she came to meet Ben Congreve, expedition leader and classicist, the man who was to have such a profound effect on her life—who was, in fact, to turn it upside down in the two short weeks of their acquaintance.

Never would she forget that first sight of him as, with others, he crouched on the sand examining the artifacts brought up that day from the sea bottom. Some remark brought a gale of laughter and he glanced up, his grin a dazzle of white against the dark face. He caught her eyes and straightened slowly, the smile fading while the dark eyes narrowed in interest. Lopped jeans and loose open shirt hid little of his sun-bronzed torso. Hair, also dark and fine, was raked back from his forehead with a touch of impatience she was to find only too characteristic.

Introductions began and his welcome had become more general, but his eyes had returned to hers, and even now, recalling the intensity of his gaze, she felt a throb of response. The world had, for that split second, halted on its axis before rushing on with the sound of an express train which only she had heard.

A beard, a shade or two lighter than his hair, had covered the lower part of his face, emphasising the faintly piratical look. The touch of natural arrogance might have been a warning. Except that those first few seconds took her far beyond the reach of warnings.

Little doubt then that on her side the attraction had been immediate and cataclysmic, and it had been an irritation that after that initial burning exchange he'd appeared to be only faintly aware of her. So many approaches by men who raised her blood pressure not a single point, and yet this man had ignored all her most blatant signals.

Afterwards, that was something he had denied hotly, laughingly assuring her he had picked her out at once, describing in detail how she had looked to him, then laughing again, grabbing her hands at that point, and pushing her back onto the sand and kissing her, teasing her, assuring her it was her swimming skill, the nearing thing to a mermaid he had seen, which had underlined his interest.

Idly she had brushed her mouth against the erotic silkiness of the dark beard, looking up through half-closed eyes. 'Of course you know the mermaid is really the manatee—the sea cow.' A heavy sigh. 'Am I supposed to be flattered.'

'Mmm.' His voice was drowsy as he pulled her closer to the curve of his body. 'The sailors were at sea a long time in those days, but, yes. You are meant to be flattered. I was talking about the mermaid of legend, the siren. That's what you reminded me of. You seem to treat the ocean like your natural element. But your skin…' He slid his palm the length of her back, his touch so sensitive it seemed every nerve-ending in her body responded. 'Your skin is like silk, and your hair…' His voice deepened to one of self-parody. 'Your hair is like gold moidores.'

She was more than ready to join in the joke, even if it was at her own expense, and her lips barely touched his, parted in a tiny giggle. 'The only ones you seem likely to encounter on this expedition. And even they are fake.'

'What?' Soporific and relaxed in the afternoon shade, with the sound of surf crashing on the distant reef and, closer, the soft, soft lap of waves on the shore all enhancing the feel of enchantment, he put his mouth on hers and murmured the drowsy question. 'What is that supposed to mean?'

She had not regretted having her long hair cropped before leaving Sydney, but the impulse which had prompted the colour change had been less successful. The pale gold did nothing for her, while sunshine and salt water on top of bleach was causing havoc. 'It means I'm all illusion, unreal.'

'Well, I really never believed in mermaids.'

While you, she assured herself in dreamy satisfaction, are the one I always believed was waiting out there for me. Somewhere. And now I've found you I mean never to let you go. With a sigh she rested her head against his chest, rubbing the warm skin, the brush of his silky hair a new and ridiculously exciting experience. 'Have you ever been to Australia, Ben?'

'No, I never have.' He mocked her faint accent. 'But

I promise, it's now top of my list of places I mean to visit.'

For a moment she detached herself, brushing some sand from the rush mat. 'What are you planning to do when you leave here?' Having been told that he and another member of the group had sailed down from Florida, she was toying with the suggestion that he might follow her to England. But they had known each other only a matter of days and he was bound to see her as trying to rush him into some kind of permanent relationship. She would do nothing to jeopardise the fragile budding attraction, and besides, she sensed something, a reticence which was hard to understand.

'We've been planning to take her—' he nodded vaguely in the direction of the yacht, which could just be glimpsed round the headland '—through the canal and into the Pacific. We have permission to spend some time on the Galapagos Islands collecting scientific data, then back up the West Coast and home.' Gazing down, he traced the outline of her mouth with his forefinger. 'One of my ambitions is to take her on a solo round-the-world, but this time Dan is coming with me. The solo will have to wait. Have you done any sailing, Helen?'

'Not really.' Regretfully she shook her head. 'In fact, not at all. In the diving club we always used power boats—much more practical than sail.'

'But much less romantic. But, look, why don't I take you out now, so you can have a look round? You might find you would want to persuade me that solo was not such a wonderful idea.'

When he pulled her to her feet and stood there, the narrowed eyes and that half-smile challenging her, she found herself hanging onto every ounce of self-control. With a rueful expression and with fingernails pressing hard into her palms she shrugged casually. 'I might. But I very much doubt it. But, since you're so keen to show off your toy…'

The rest of that lazy afternoon they spent diving from the deck of the small sleek yacht into the shimmering clear water, and when the sun began to dip below the horizon they settled on towels spread on the deck, deliciously idle, occasionally sipping ice-cold drinks, watching as the ocean gleamed with every fiery colour in the spectrum.

'Well, what do you think?' Ben, perched on one elbow reached out to touch the back of her hand, stirring fine sensitive hairs and a thousand barely controlled emotions. 'You ready to come beachcombing with me?'

'Mmm.' Impossible for her to speak when she was fighting to understand why that particular touch…light as a moth's wing…should… Yes. She wanted to yell aloud. Yes, please. But she knew enough to recognise a rhetorical question when she met it, and had no wish to embarrass him. Or herself. How devastating if she were to agree then have him back off. Besides, for this moment it was enough to be with him as she was now. And to know that if *he* showed the least sign of wanting to go further, there would be no holding back.

As if sensing her feelings, he leaned over then and touched his mouth to hers, murmuring her name in a tone of such frustrated longing that she had no further thought of restraint. Her lips parted for him, hands twisting in his hair as she pulled his weight down.

'Helen, you've no idea…' His voice was low and hurried, and for the first time she was aware of sexual power. 'You've no idea how I feel.'

At that she allowed herself a faint smile, and watched through half-closed eyes as she passed fingertips over the warm contours of his torso. Her voice was consciously sultry. 'What makes you think I don't know?'

'You know where this is going to lead?' His dark eyes had a heady, slumbrous look, and their entwined bodies were dark-gilded by the setting sun.

'Mmm. What is there to stop us?' Her heart was hammering against her chest. Or was it his?

'Is it all right?' The significance of that query occurred to her much later, but she knew that even fully aware her answer would have been the same.

Begrudging every inch that separated them, she reached up, biting gently but with fierce impatience on his lower lip. 'Everything will be all right, if only...' And in an attack of sudden modesty she murmured against his ear.

And he laughed. A deep, growly sound which resonated in his chest, primitive and satisfying in a way she could not describe and which she could never forget.

It was hard, at this distance, to understand how they had been able to keep their affair from the others during the next few days. Possibly because they had been similarly preoccupied, and it had not occurred to either Helen or Ben to flaunt what they'd felt for each other. Or at least what *she'd* felt. Time seemed to prove that for Ben Congreve it had been little more than a holiday romance, passionate and exciting while it lasted, a very enjoyable interlude, but one that was easily forgotten once he sailed off to another continent. To another life—where he had a fiancée waiting, the preacher booked and the wedding gown ordered.

But of course she had known nothing of those when he had first made gentle and skilful love to her, nor on the subsequent nights, when things had grown still more intense and passionate. And even if she *had* known, she was uncertain the knowledge would have been a deterrent.

It had been a long time before she was able to admit as much—after she had passed through periods of desolation and anguish. Only then was she honest enough to admit that nothing would have kept her from him. And in one way at least she had never regretted it. Oh, for heaven's sake, why be coy? There was no way she regretted what had been the definitive experience of her life.

But that was not to say she hadn't been deeply wounded when, one evening after he had sailed off, after all his promises, she'd overheard the casual conversation between two of the American girls who had known him well.

'Yeah.' The tall blonde straightened up from the bowl where she was scrubbing at the deposits on some old pottery lids. 'In the fall, I understand. They have known each other for ever and Ben's parents are delighted with the engagement. She's a year or two younger—about twenty-three or four—and filthy rich, of course. But those are the circles they move in, so I imagine…'

Unwilling to hear any more, Helen walked away, eyes filmed with misery, throat choked as she stared over the ocean, that same glorious expanse of water which had shielded them, which had absorbed their cries of pleasure.

The pressure in her chest was causing real pain. So, this was what it was all about, that first slight reticence, the avoidance of so many personal details, no offer of an address or telephone number where he could be contacted. He had taken her parents' Sydney number with the assurance that her London address would soon be available, and what was it he had murmured in her ear just before they said goodbye?

'I shall be with you just as soon as I can... Just one or two problems to be sorted out and I shall be on a flight. No chance of sailing—much too slow.'

So, she had stood on the headland until the last tiny patch of sale had vanished from the horizon, confident and happy that soon they would be together again. And even after overhearing that conversation she didn't lose hope. She was simply impatient to be done with this stupid diving exercise so she could find herself an address in London. Where she could wait for his call to bring an end to this agonising uncertainty. Nothing else in the world mattered to her.

CHAPTER TWO

SINGAPORE the following day was as frantic and fascinating as Ellie remembered. She and Jenny spent a diverting morning drifting round the prestigious stores and the more ethnic boutiques, buying this and that. Several presents were bought for Charlie and friends at home, then, after lunch at Raffles, they were driven, exhausted, back to the apartment.

'It is just so hot.' Jenny sighed with relief as they walked into the air-conditioned rooms, going straight to the space-age kitchen, reaching into the refrigerator for a jug of fresh orange juice. She filled two glasses, one of which she handed to Ellie. 'I suggest we have a siesta in preparation for this evening.'

'This evening?' Ellie, who was deeply weary, stifled a yawn. 'What do you mean? Don't forget I'm on an early flight tomorrow.'

'That is exactly why I'm suggesting a rest this afternoon. Tonight we eat out, maybe dance. You see—' she strolled back to the salon, Ellie in her wake '—we've been invited out to one of the newer nightspots.'

'I hope this hasn't been laid on for my benefit, Jenny. I wouldn't have thought Robert was all that keen. In fact, last night I heard him say his idea of a perfect evening was to spend it at home alone…'

'I hope he didn't say that exactly. If he did then our guests might have taken it as a hint for them to leave early…'

'Which is exactly what they did not do.' Ellie laughed. 'No, Robert was more diplomatic about it. In fact, I think he said ''alone with a few friends''—which is most likely why they all hung on till gone midnight.'

'Mmm. Well, Robert is nothing if not diplomatic—though he can be very ruthless too when the mood takes him.' She paused, walked to the mirror above the side table and fiddled with a jade earring. She was studiedly casual. 'What did you think of Ben Congreve?'

'Ben Congreve?' The mere mention of the name she had been trying to forget brought her out in a cold sweat, heart hammering loud enough to be heard across the room. 'Oh, he seemed pleasant enough.' She was immediately struck by the banality of the description for such a man—it was sure to make Jenny suspicious. 'Oh, more than that, I would say a very interesting man.'

'But not interesting enough for you, Ellie?' It was a carefully judged question, and without turning her head Ellie was aware of her friend's close scrutiny. 'Now, I wonder why that should be?' Jenny's ridiculously high heels tap-tapped on the marble floor as she strolled to join her friend at the window. 'I wonder why that should be, my dear? I would have thought most women would have immediately been struck by him.'

'And what about you?' Time for a diversionary tactic. 'Are you one of those knocked sideways by the famous writer?' Her smile, the teasing expression, were indications that they were engaged in an amusing game, nothing more.

'At one time,' Jenny confessed, hands outspread to show she was concealing nothing, 'I might easily have been, but now I am in what looks like being a permanent and very constant relationship. Whereas you…'

'Whereas I—' deliberately she copied Jenny's apologetic and self-mocking gesture '—I have Charlie.' And what, she asked silently, did Ben Congreve know about constant relationships? The thought, the words she had so often used as explanation and excuse, combined to make her feel as if a large rock had invaded her chest. 'And I'm not in the market for any kind of relationship right now, permanent or casual.' Especially the latter, since she knew exactly how much heartbreak would ensue.

'Mmm.' Jenny's non-committal expression was clearly sceptical, but she was disinclined to pursue the subject. 'Anyway, I shall send Ay Leng to your room with some tea, then you can have an hour or two to prepare for the evening. 'Oh...' She grimaced as she stepped out of her shoes. 'My poor feet... Robert tells me I ought not to torture myself with such high heels, but if they were lower, no one would notice me.'

'That,' Ellie grinned, 'is something I find very hard to believe.'

'Well...' Jenny shrugged, raising dark, elegant eyebrows. 'Forget about me and tell me what you're going to wear this evening. If any of your clothes need pressing, one of the maids...'

'No problem about that. Most of what I have with me has already been whisked away by some invisible hand, dealt with and returned to the wardrobe. Dinner and dance, you say.' Ellie frowned over the poverty of her choice. 'I think last night almost exhausted my selection. I didn't expect to be going out two nights in succession.' It seemed appropriate to emphasise the dullness of her life with a joke.

'I've already told you what I think of that.' Jenny had

indeed expressed her opinion forcefully on more than one occasion. 'I know all about your wonderful rapport with Charlie, but still, it's time you got out and about a whole lot more...'

'Tell me what to wear.' Ellie regretted having provoked a lecture on that subject, especially today, and determined to change the direction of the conversation. 'Better still, tell me what you are going to wear—that will give me some idea. I do have a floaty cotton skirt and a camisole top, if you think that would be any good.'

Five minutes later, with the matter decided, Ellie was left alone in the bedroom, only too glad of the chance to lie back on her bed, eyes closed, and try to blot from her mind all thoughts of the man who had so unexpectedly come back into her life. And she was at least partly successful, for although his image was firmly etched on the underside of her eyelids—the old Ben Congreve, bearded and piratical, rather than the new cleanshaven svelte version—the scenes she was reviewing were happy ones.

There was a bittersweet pleasure in reliving those early enchanted days, and kindly sleep overcame her before the cruel memories intruded. Though when she woke, her cheeks were damp.

'You look wonderful, Ellie.' Jenny, an exotic firefly in a brilliantly coloured cheongsam, had no idea that her very presence made the most sophisticated western woman feel clumsy and inadequate, turned with an enquiring look when she heard her friend laugh.

'Compared with you, I feel drab and colourless. And I think most people would agree with me. Shall we ask Robert to judge?' she asked as her host came in.

'No, best not.' Jenny grinned. 'I think you're entirely wrong, but it would be unfair to put him to the test. I daren't risk it,' she quipped with total self-assurance. 'Ready, darling?'

'Yes, the car is waiting. You both look extremely decorative.' And he was surprised when they giggled.

The drive in the stretch limo through the pulsating city streets took them to a small smart nightclub overlooking the ocean, and even as they drew up in front of the vestibule, the setting, the subdued lighting, the erotic rhythms of the music wakened in Ellie long-suppressed inclinations. There was a sudden desire to be young, to respond as she once had, carefree and uninhibited.

So it was with anticipation that she followed Robert, who was being guided by the head waiter, among the tables towards a secluded alcove at the far side of the restaurant. The smile on her lips faltered when, on their approach, Ben Congreve rose to his feet to greet them. And since it was towards her his eyes were drawn, she was sure her reaction must have been noted.

'Robert, Jenny…' He welcomed them and there was the slightest hesitation before he spoke Ellie's name, a hint of uncertainty which confirmed her suspicion, though it might have been simply that he was trying to gauge her attitude and his own. As it was, he chose informality, something Ellie appreciated as she shook hands with the three people already sitting round the table.

'Jenny, Robert, you already know everyone, but, Ellie, may I introduce Darren and Myra Gottlieb from the American Consulate? And this—' he indicated the tall, good-looking man who had the air of a local '—is Danny Khim, who is with my publisher.'

It was disconcerting to find when they all sat down once again that she was next to Ben with Danny on her left. Not at all what she would have chosen…but there was little she could do about it. She tried to compose herself, to ignore the feeling of being manipulated by Jenny as much as by Ben Congreve, and allowed the conversation to pass her by while she wrestled with her emotions. But she was too conscious of the man on her right to be entirely successful, even imagined she was picking up vibes from his body—sheer nonsense, of course. Meantime she endeavoured to be fascinated by Jenny's conversation with Danny, until Ben spoke, that was, and then it was impossible to ignore him.

'So, Ellie, tell me what you've been doing today.' He was so very smooth and commanding, so very Ivy League, as he always had been. But she was less impressionable than she once had been, had spent years on her guard and had honed her self-protection to a fine edge. And certainly she was too old to imagine that fine clothes and manners meant anything, which explained why she chose to adopt a sarcastic drawl.

'Oh, the usual touristy things—you know, a few souvenirs to take home, lunch at Raffles. Certainly nothing which compares with researching a new bestseller.'

Though his expression barely changed, something about him suggested chagrin. 'Oh, I don't know, I always find choosing one or two gifts to take home is a pleasant enough task. I positively enjoy finding things my friends will appreciate.' His eyes were searching, as if trying to find a softer woman than the chippy one he had seen so far. 'And what makes you think researching a book is so diverting? There are times when it is sheer grind. Besides, weren't you doing a little research of your own last night?'

'I was?' Impossible to think what he meant, especially when he had decided to switch on the charm. His warmth gave no clue to his real character, she thought meanly…

'Sure. Didn't I hear you say you must try to remember all the colours of that Corot painting in the salon?'

'Oh, that.' Of course, she had joked about it with Babs but had been unaware of him overhearing. 'I must confess I do that all the time. I have a compulsive interest in colour.'

'Well, as I said…' When he smiled, as he was doing now, it was difficult to hang on to her stand-offish manner. Besides, what did it matter? It seemed to her that he was their host for the evening, and she owed it to Robert and Jenny. It would cost her nothing to be polite, since once the evening was over they would never meet again. With luck. That assurance was less of a comfort than she would have wished.

The food and wine were delicious, and she found herself relaxed to the extent that when Danny asked, she allowed herself to be persuaded onto the dance floor. Mainly it was to escape from Ben Congreve, with his endless questions, and when they returned to the table she took the chance to change seats—easy enough since Robert alone wasn't dancing. In different circumstances she knew she would have enjoyed herself, but the night was too fraught with the possibility that Ben might ask her to dance—and how could she refuse?

In the event, when he did make his move, her mind went blank, excuses evaporated and she found herself being led away from the others, not even trying to detach her fingers from his. Perhaps it was down to the music, calming and very nearly soporific. Who could feel threatened cocooned in such bittersweet nostalgia, rather than the pulsing rhythms of previous numbers? On the other hand, it was not the mood she would have chosen to share with him. Calm detachment was what she would have liked to help combat these…these sensations flowing between them.

'I'm still waiting to hear about *you* Ellie.' Cradling her hand more comfortably, he looked down, and their linked fingers brushing accidentally against the round swell of her breast brought her heart leaping into her throat.

And she knew she had been wrong to wear this wispy silk camisole. It was impossibly revealing, and she knew it showed every curve of the bare skin beneath, plus a fair amount of cleavage. She could hardly believe she had worn it without its usual overblouse, and certainly it hadn't been for his benefit since she hadn't known…

Her breath was growing more agitated now, emphasising all the aspects she would have liked to conceal, and he must be aware of the increase in her pulse-rate. His hand on her back could hardly avoid the signals, would know how little she was wearing and would draw his own conclusions.

A deep breath to control her trembling, and when she found her voice, it sounded gratifyingly calm and matter-of-fact. 'There's so little to tell. You must know it all already.' This was her usual glib evasion of a 'tell all' invitation, but her resolve was undermined when she looked up into those searching dark eyes. How right she had been to be wary. Writer's eyes, she decided sarcastically, forever trying to find copy for his novels. As bad as the paparazzi, always probing into personal secrets for financial gain. 'And mostly so very boring,' she finished.

A certain amount of truth in that. So many years huddling over a knitting machine added little sparkle to one's personality, especially when all one's contemporaries had been out doing the clubs.

'That I find hard to believe.'

'No, I promise you.' Reluctantly she dragged her eyes away, looking about her with an air of determined and slightly desperate enjoyment, searching for some banal comment and failing, resisting his attempts to pull her closer, then feeling foolish when there was a near collision with another couple.

Easy to interpret that raised eyebrow as speaking volumes. No, he was assuring her, I'm not the least bit interested, so don't let your imagination run riot. And she blushed spectacularly as if she had been truly reprimanded, then was startled when his amused voice did interrupt her thoughts.

'Do you come here often?' It was an attempt at humour which deserved no reply but he was persistent. 'Now it's your turn to say something. I have asked you if you come here often, now you must make some remark about, say, the music, or—' An abrupt stop as again he apologised to another couple—an excuse to hold her closer for a second.

But it was hard to remain aloof when he was speaking so like a character from her beloved Jane Austen. She glanced up in mocking reproach. 'You stepped on my foot, Mr Congreve.' Then it was too much for her, she smiled, and her whole personality was illuminated, transformed.

'There.' It was a moment before Ben spoke, a moment when his eyes held hers with dismaying warmth. 'Just as I was about to give up. But I knew I could amuse you in the end. Despite your prejudice.' Then, as her expression darkened again, he burst into laughter. 'You're not going to pretend, Ellie, that you haven't been trying to take me down a peg? Just like Lizzie Bennett with Mr Darcy.'

'You are quite mistaken.'

'You will never convince me.' The music ended and they returned to their table, his touch on her arm more possessive than she would have liked. 'But I would like to know why.'

'As I said, you have made a mistake.'

'If you insist, I shan't press you.' There was a slight hold-up on the edge of the dance floor. 'But I mean to find out in the end.' His eyes narrowed assessingly. She had the impression of him trying to bore into her soul. 'I have a habit of getting my own way eventually.'

'Of that, Mr Congreve,' she said, and now her voice was icy with fear and, yes, with dislike, 'I have not the faintest doubt. People like you...' But fortunately at that moment the path was cleared and she took the chance to sweep past him and to rejoin the company.

'Always do?' he suggested coolly as they sat down, but she turned her shoulder and was glad when he took the hint and for the rest of the evening left her in peace.

As they were whisked back to the apartment Ellie had only half of her attention on the animated conversation as Jenny enthused about the evening's events.

At least he had not had the effrontery to ask her to dance again. And she *wasn't* aggrieved over that. She saw no contradiction in her thoughts, although many women would have felt resentment. Three times he had asked Jenny to dance, Myra twice. But who was counting? And she had quite deliberately gone off to the powder room round about midnight when she had thought he might be mellowing towards her again.

No, on the whole she was pleased with the way she had coped with what had been a fraught situation, and the fact that now she felt like howling with misery was due to a whole series of things—mostly to do with change of climate and fatigue, and missing Charlie of course, and nothing—well, be honest—at least very little to do with being held close to Ben Congreve.

Strangely enough she was able to recuperate to an extent on the flight home, spending much of it with her eyes closed, not wholly asleep but with her brain in neutral, and Ben Congreve absent but for that vague and persistent pain in her chest. But it was time to move on, put all that behind her, and it was especially comforting when she touched down at Heathrow to find David Merriman waiting for her.

'Bless you.' Wonderful to have a kind, undemanding man to heave her luggage in the back of the car, to be relieved of any transport worries as they drove through the capital's clogged arteries. 'You're a sight for sore eyes. I thought you'd be on call today.' With a sigh she leaned her head back against the seat and turned to look at his familiar profile. 'How did you manage to swing it?'

'Oh, I can usually manage to get away when I particularly want to. I did an extra surgery at the weekend and Harry is seeing my patients today so you needn't worry.'

'I'm glad.' Ellie slid lower in her seat. 'Now, tell me

what's been happening at home over the past week. When I spoke to Charlie the other day all appeared to be as usual.'

'Pretty much, I should say. But Charlie will be glad to see you back again.'

'That makes two of us.' After that the conversation became general as he passed on the few items of village gossip. Mrs Gatherley's baby, she learned, had appeared four weeks ahead of schedule and Kyle James had broken his arm falling off the climbing frame in his garden.

'So...' She smiled at him. 'Our revered GP is being kept as busy as ever.'

'Alas,' he sighed. 'But not so busy I haven't had time to miss you as well. Charlie isn't the only one who has been counting the days.'

'That's sweet of you, David.' But, sadly, her feelings for him were as ambivalent as ever. How simple life would be if she could make a sensible, obvious choice, forget the distraction of Ben Congreve and...

'I have tickets for a concert on Friday, and of course I'm hoping you'll come with me.'

'Oh, Friday?' Her search for an excuse was automatic. 'I'm not sure... I have so much time to make up...so many things I must do...'

'I'm hoping you'll at least try...'

'Of course I'll try, David.' How could she be so ungracious when he did so much for her? 'I'll do my best, but if I find I can't, then what about Liz?' David's sister was also his housekeeper.

'I think it does us both good to have a break from each other.' He negotiated the exit from the motorway and soon they were on the very minor road which led to their village of Little Transome. 'But don't worry, if you decide you can't, I have a friend whom I know will enjoy it.'

Ellie was feeling guilty. He was such a kind man, a great GP, and, she feared, just waiting for the green light which would signify a formal courtship. It was with relief that she saw the gates at the end of her drive and reached down for her handbag. But before the car had even stopped in front of the mellow stone-built house, the front door was thrown back and a small figure threw herself down the few steps.

'Mummy, Mummy.' A mini-tornado draped itself around Ellie, hands round her neck, legs about her waist. 'I've missed you such a lot. It's been so awful without you.'

'And I've missed you too, Charlie.' She laughed, sniffed, blinked away a tendency to tears. 'But I can't imagine it's been too awful when Wendy's been looking after you.'

Over the child's head she directed an apologetic glance towards the young woman who stood smiling and shaking her head at the top of the steps. Wendy Cummings had been with her since Charlie was a toddler, had held the fort on innumerable occasions when she had been forced to go off on business trips. Without her, Ellie could hardly have carried on—certainly IGRAINE Woollens would not have progressed as it had done over the last few years... It was a relief to see Wendy shrug forgivingly as well, safe in the knowledge that for most of the time she and Charlie were the best of friends.

'Come on then, poppet.' With an arm about the small shoulders, she led the way inside, followed by David, who dumped her cases in the hall and returned to the car to retrieve the collection of packages. They walked together into the kitchen. 'Am I glad to be back, Wendy.'

'Hectic trip?' Wendy swung round from the Aga with a tray of scones.

'You could say...' Then, laughing at the insistent questioning of her daughter, 'No, I didn't forget. If you go and ask David for the large blue bag you can see what's inside. And tell him Wendy has the kettle on, so if he would like a cup of tea and one of her scones he should come straight through.'

'I won't, thanks, Ellie.' The doctor's head poked round the kitchen door. 'I think you'll have enough on for the rest of the day, but I'll call you about Friday. See what you think when you've had time to relax.'

When she had seen him drive off towards the village, Ellie returned to the kitchen with a feeling of release, in time to see Charlie for once very nearly speechless as she gazed at the beautifully dressed Siamese doll Ellie had brought from Hong Kong.

'Oh, Mummy, thank you. She is so gorgeous.'

'Well, she's just another one for your collection—oh, and all her clothes come off too. And if you pick up that pink bag and give it to Wendy, I think she deserves a present too, for looking after you so well.'

'Yes, she does.' And when the package was opened, the silk blouse drooled over, they all sat down round the large kitchen table drinking tea and eating hot buttered scones and strawberry jam while Ellie entertained them with the highlights of her trip.

Except...except that one highlight wasn't mentioned. She omitted the minor fact that while there she had, for the first time since her conception, met the man who was

Charlie's father. Little point in bringing that up, since everyone was under the impression that Charlie's father had died soon after she had been born, and, more to the point, that her real father had not the slightest notion of her existence. And if she, Ellie Osborne, had anything to do with it then he never would. It was so obvious that he did not care.

Men who embarked so casually on affairs and promptly forgot them were simply contemptible. And she was far too proud ever to confess to being one in a long line of lovers of any man. Even of one as rich and famous as 'Jonas Parnell' had become. A line so lengthy that he had no recollection of her existence. It was hard to think of anything more humiliating.

CHAPTER THREE

AMAZING how quickly life could return to normal. That at least was the comforting message Ellie fixed her mind on at night before falling asleep, but waking, as she did now, in the early hours brought an entirely different perspective.

Now, tossing and turning in a frustration she did not care to identify, she knew life could never be quite as simple again. That, having met Ben Congreve, it was impossible for her to convince herself as she had done before that their affair had been a pretty typical holiday romance, something which in any event would not have lasted.

And there was one vital matter she forced herself to face: She must admit at last that the blame could not be placed entirely at his door. So mad had she been for him she had assured him, quite without foundation, that there was no risk of pregnancy. Over the years she had convinced herself that he had allowed her to lie to him...well, that was what suited most men, wasn't it?

But how frightening it had all been, finding herself alone, pregnant, deserted. Looking back, it was hard to imagine how she had pulled herself together, to plan for some kind of future. It had been her great good fortune to meet Greg Osborne and marry him, and, of course, the greatest good fortune of all was Charlie herself. Charlie, who had brought more love and joy into her life than she could have imagined. That one shining fact made any kind of regret redundant.

Only…meeting him again now threatened all the feelings and emotions kept so carefully damped down over the years. Even now, her relationship with David Merriman was a tentative, arm's length one, no matter that he had made it clear he would like it to develop into something warmer. And Ellie was afraid even that prospect must now be consigned to the dustbin.

'Oh…' She groaned, put her head beneath the covers, desperately trying to restore sleep before the image of Ben Congreve intruded again, but it was impossible. For how could she pretend to herself that if they had met as strangers at the dinner date in Singapore she would not have been interested? And the fact that he had showed so clearly that he was interested too…that simply made it more difficult.

Oh, it had all been more restrained and civilised than all those years before, but that was natural—they were older, less abandoned than that group of sexually experimental youngsters had been. And it had taught her a crucial lesson: she was very much more wary, less trusting, but still… If only they had been meeting for the first time and both free… But, there, that would imply that Charlie…

Oh, it was all too tormenting and she wished they hadn't met up after all, was glad—positively—that nothing had come of it, and… And, oh, how she longed for sleep.

So, it was something of a surprise, mixed undeniably with a surge of sheer pleasure, to answer the door late on Saturday afternoon and find Ben Congreve standing there. So wholly unexpected she could feel the blood leave her head, was forced to hang onto the door handle for dear life.

'Hi, Ellie.' A touch of reserve, uncertainty, perhaps, in such a normally assured man. 'Remember me?' Remember him indeed! 'I've been trying to call you all day but couldn't get a reply.'

'No, well...' Little choice but to hold wide the door, inviting him into the hall. She was pleased it looked its highly polished best, with a bowl of cream roses spilling onto the dark oak table... 'I've been shopping all day and have just come back. I think I might have forgotten to switch on the machine.'

'I hope you don't mind me calling, but...' Another trace of diffidence as the dark gaze searched for contrary signs. 'Since I was almost passing your door I thought I'd risk it.'

'No, of course not.' Ellie, with every appearance of calm, led him into the drawing room, thinking of the friends who were due round for supper, trying not to panic as she thought of all she had to do before then. 'But...you were passing the door, you say?' Her tone, though still light and friendly, was unmistakably sceptical.

'Almost. Jenny gave me your address before I left Singapore, and when I realised—'

'She did?' Now disapproval added to her doubts.

'I persuaded her, I'm afraid.' His expression was guarded. 'So, if you object, you must blame me, not Jenny.'

'But why should I object?' Turning aside was a protective gesture. 'Would you like some tea? A drink, perhaps...?'

'Only if you're going to have some too. Tea sounds wonderful.'

'I shan't be a minute.'

But he followed her into the kitchen, hesitating in the doorway when he saw the large round table spread with a dark blue cloth, places laid for five—all accomplished by Wendy before she whisked Charlie off to spend the weekend at her cottage.

'Oh, I can see I have called at the wrong time. Listen, forget the tea. You're having company round, so...'

'No.' Perversely, she had no intention of allowing him to go off, doubtless feeling unwelcome, possibly even reporting to Jenny that the English were a cold, stand-offish race. She wished he had not come, but she smiled, pushed the kettle onto the hot plate of the Aga and reached for the teapot. 'It won't take a minute. Besides, everything is under control.'

And then, unexpectedly, her brain was toying with a wild idea. If it had been any other casual caller she would have thought nothing of asking him to make up numbers—since Andrew had dropped out she was short of a man. If it hadn't been for their...relationship, what more natural than to ask him to join the party? It wasn't often Little Transome had the chance of sharing a meal with a bestselling author—the others would be thrilled. Perhaps she owed it to them.

'You were saying?' She poured tea, emptied some biscuits onto a plate and led him to the table in the window where he could enjoy the view. 'You were in the area?' A raised eyebrow commented on the least likely scenario anyone could have imagined.

'Mmm.' A piece of shortbread vanished in one bite and he reached out for another. 'My publisher lives near

Amberley. I had lunch with him and then it seemed a shame not to give ourselves a second chance at friendship.' Now his attention was on her face. Impossible for him to miss the wave of scarlet which overwhelmed her, and she took evasive action by fetching the teapot to refill the cups.

'Yes, well...'

'I did hope to persuade you to come to dinner in the Red Cow tonight. I booked into the local pub with that particular idea in mind.'

'Well...' Now she was on firm ground, was able to produce the perfect excuse. 'I couldn't have gone in any case. I have a daughter, you see.' *Your* daughter, in fact, was a silent accusation. Her colour had returned to normal, making it possible for her to study him with cool detachment. At least, she hoped that was the impression she was giving, for inside all her emotions raged.

'Yes.' He drained his cup, sat back in his chair, one forefinger crooked against his mouth. 'Yes, Jenny told me. It must be tough bringing up a child on your own.'

Ellie said nothing, simply sat there looking at him, making a mental note to have a few words with Jenny.

'She told me too you are a widow. I'm afraid I pressed her once again.' He shrugged. 'I had an excuse—I wanted to get to know you better.' He didn't say it was these facts which had persuaded him to come but he watched her reactions closely, seeing her colour come and go in the most provocative way. She looked little more than a child herself, with her hair tied back like that.

Again Ellie felt the heat in her face, but decided to take the attack to him. 'So, you're still gathering information on me while I have no means of finding out more about you? Apart from being told you are a famous writer—' she hoped she was giving the impression of never having heard of Jonas Parnell '—I know nothing about you. So…I'm assuming since you must be about…what?…thirty-two? that you must…'

'Exactly right.' She must remember to be more careful. 'So, what do you want to know, Ellie? You have only to ask. If you're wondering if I'm married…'

'No, I hadn't even thought of it.' But her protest was too sharp to be convincing and he grinned amiably.

'Well, that's really disappointing, but as it happens my marriage is past tense. Divorced about a year ago, and that was kinda tough.'

'Oh.' Pity you weren't so scrupulous in the past, she accused silently, when you were simply engaged and forgot about it. On the other hand, there was no reason to be pleased with what he had just said—in fact it meant nothing to her at all except as a matter of interest. Other people's lives were inevitably more interesting than one's own. 'I can believe that. And especially if there were children.'

'No children were involved, so…' Did he sigh? 'I suppose that ought to have been a relief.' His manner implied the opposite. 'But I like kids.'

And the only one you have is the one you will never know about.

'And where is your daughter, Ellie? What's her name, by the way?'

'Her name is Charlie.' Deliberately she turned away. There was something so wounding about this conversation with this man, but even out of vision he would not be other than throbbingly present. 'Short for Charlotte, which she hates, or says she does.'

'I wonder why? It's such a pretty name.'

'Before she went to school all her friends were boys, and I think that was her way of keeping up with them. Now no one ever calls her anything but Charlie and she's delighted.' Smiling tenderly, she turned without thinking and encountered his searching glance. 'And she's with a friend right now, sleeping over since I'm busy fixing supper. But I mustn't bore you, running on like a doting mother.'

'You're not boring me a bit, but—' he stood, stretching slightly, as if he had had a long day and was tired '—I can see I'm in your way and you have lots to do. But I'm going to be in England for a few days and I'm hoping we can meet up. Since that first day I've been determined we ought to know each other better.'

'The first day?' She frowned, confused for a moment into speaking rashly.

'That very first moment at Robert's apartment. I knew I wanted to meet you again. In spite of the fact that you were sending all kinds of discouraging signals.'

'I wasn't,' she lied, this time without blushing.

That raised an eyebrow. 'Well, you could have fooled me. At first I took it that you were warning me off because you were married—I did just notice the rings. Then, when Jenny told me your husband had died a long time ago, I reckoned maybe you had got into the habit of discouraging close relationships…'

'Close relationships?' Now was the time to put a spoke in this wheel; her own safety was at stake. 'In my mind, those have to develop very slowly, over years.' Not what she had once thought, of course. 'So it's hardly likely to happen over the few days you're in England.'

'No, but a guy has to make a start somewhere, and I

was hoping that if you and Charlie would like to come up to London for a day then maybe we could make a start.'

'Ben...' It was the first time she had used his name, and it was spoken in a tone of patient tolerance and detachment which pleased her. 'I can't imagine what else Jenny said to you—I don't discuss my personal affairs with even close friends—but for all you, or she, might know, I could be in what you call a "close relationship" at the moment. In which case you might very easily be wasting your time.'

'I would never consider it to be that. Even if the outcome were to be the wrong one from my point of view.'

His gaze was dominating—sexually dominating, she thought indignantly, but when had it been otherwise? Dominating and weakening, so it was easy to understand exactly why she had been so pliable when they'd first met. He took a step closer, reached out a hand, tilting her face upwards so it was impossible to avoid his scrutiny.

'There is something about you I don't understand, Ellie, something which intrigues me. That...that almost haunted look could be explained by your husband's death—it must have hit you hard—but...it's more than that. It's as if you've been on the defensive for a long time, and—'

'I don't think we ought to go on with this session of amateur psychology, do you?' This was too close for comfort. Releasing herself, she took a step backwards, reaching round to adjust a pot on top of the Aga. 'Besides, you're misreading the entire situation. I assure you, I'm perfectly happy and fulfilled. I have a daughter who is the centre of my life, a successful business that

keeps me busy and brings great rewards, and, as well—'
she waved a hand towards the table, as if that explained
the rest of her life '—I have a circle of friends who fill
my social life more than adequately.'

Now she was feeling angry at his determined intru-
sion, and perhaps even more at her own response, which
was much less detached than she would have liked. 'But
if you're still curious, then why don't you join us for
supper? Nothing elaborate, you understand. But then you
can really assure yourself that I am truly fulfilled in
every aspect of my life.' She gave a tiny, condescending
smile. 'Though I doubt that is what you want to see. I
am almost resigned to identifying myself in your next
bestseller as the frustrated mature woman who doesn't
know what she's missing in life till the hero turns up
and shows her exactly what has gone wrong.'

For a few seconds they glared, then he spoke with a
barely subdued lilt of amusement. 'I'm not sure you've
got my genre right, but...frustrated? That is a word
which in no way describes you. Nor mature. I'm sure
you're not a day over twenty-four. But, as to the plot,
well, maybe you have something which could persuade
me to change my style. That kind of happy ending ap-
peals to most ages, though I can't see such a scene in
anything I have planned at the moment. I guess maybe
these things happen more in real life than in fiction, and
if you've read anything by Jonas Parnell—'

'I haven't.' Mean of her to speak with such triumphant
haste.

'Well, I can't say I blame you for that, but I don't
have the habit of using my friends as fodder, so I can
promise you won't see yourself as the prototype for one
of my characters any more than I shall. Anyway, you

invited me to come for supper, and if you're sure I shan't be intruding then I shall be very happy to accept. Only I shan't promise not to use the scene at some time in the future. I'm sure a group of friends having supper in this perfect English setting could be intriguing—so many emotions simmering under the surface the way the meal is simmering in the oven...'

'I should forget that. It's been done to death, according to what I read of book reviews. And life isn't exactly a simmering cauldron here in Little Transome—more a wholesome plate of roast beef and Yorkshire pudding with just a touch of horseradish to add some zest.' The simile rather pleased her, reminding her of the light-hearted discussions they'd used to have, only... 'Well—' it was time to be brisk '—I shall look forward to seeing you later, and in the meantime...'

But when he had gone, returning to the room he had booked at the Red Cow, Ellie felt her assumed confidence vanish like a puff of smoke. She sank down onto the hall chair, pressed her hands together to control their shaking, and faced the realisation that she must be crazy. How could she have invited him here for a meal? She *knew* that having anything to do with Ben Congreve was playing with fire.

Her mind raced in circles, trying to find an escape route. Ought she to send a message to the pub saying she had been struck down with some crippling illness? Food poisoning would perhaps be enough to send him scuttling back to the States in panic.

But deep, deep down, underneath all the pretence of disillusion, was a shaft of pleasure that she could still attract a man like Ben Congreve. And—why not admit it?—even a tiny sense of satisfaction that she could respond, that the feminine emotions long suppressed had not entirely atrophied, and for that she was glad. It was one thing to hold aloof from that sort of thing, quite another to know no one else was interested.

So, for a little while she would go along with what had happened, but merely as a means of testing her character. This time she knew she could trust herself—no chance of her falling into his hands like a ripe plum. Not this time. It might even be that Ellie Osborne was the one woman Ben Congreve would remember simply because she was the one he could not pull.

But how awful to be like that. The idea filled her with both pity and distaste. She had thought only pop stars and lechers came into that category—those who had shared a bed with so many, the faces of most had disappeared into the crowd.

A wave of anger hit her—anger with herself and her youthful naïveté, burning anger against him for such lack of integrity. No one meeting him now would ever believe... And yet wasn't that the stock in trade of such men? To present such an honourable public face, it was bound to make seduction so easy.

Impatient with herself for allowing her mind to dwell on all that was painful in her past, she forced herself from the chair and into the kitchen, began rinsing the cups they had used under the hot tap, glad that ahead of her lay so many tasks which would keep her thoughts away from the distraction of Ben Congreve and his affairs.

But it was only a few minutes later, when she was carrying some plates across to the Aga, ready to be placed in the warming oven, that the idea suddenly occurred to her. And was as suddenly dismissed. However fair and just it might seem, there was no way she was prepared to give Ben Congreve the green light and then...then in the most cruel way, to switch on the red. Tempting as it might be to exact retribution...she simply did not have the stomach for it.

CHAPTER FOUR

BECAUSE of Ben Congreve, his inconvenient visit and the time-wasting thoughts he had provoked, Ellie was well behind with her preparations and had time only for a very hasty shower rather than the leisurely bath she had planned. She was, in fact, literally applying her make-up as, from the bedroom window, she saw the first car turn in through the gates at the far end of the drive. A second to flick a comb through her hair—luckily she had visited the hairdresser just yesterday—a blast of Givenchy and she was at the door as David and Liz came up the steps.

Because there was just a hint of autumn chill in the evening air, Ellie had decided to put a match to the logs in the dog-grate, and now flames were crackling merrily.

'Wonderful to see a fire.' Liz held out her hands to the warmth. 'A bit early for me—I hate all the dust and try to put it off as long as possible—but I do love them. Nothing else gives that same comfort. Oh, thank you, Ellie.' She took one of the long-stemmed glasses being offered, then, as the door knocker rapped, said, 'Oh, go and answer that, David.' She caught her brother as he was about to subside onto one of the sofas. 'Save Ellie's legs—it will be Clive and Tanya, or...'

'No, it's all right.' Ellie had recently found herself resenting the way David allowed his sister to boss him around, and certainly did not intend to allow it here in her own home. 'Besides it might not be—'

But before she had time to put down her tray, David was crossing the hall. 'I *have* invited someone else...' she began in mild reproof, but almost at once she recognised the voices of the neighbors Liz had mentioned. She was struck at the same time by another thought. If David could give the impression of being very much at home, then surely that would serve a powerful purpose. She had hinted to Ben Congreve that she was not without friends of the opposite sex, so maybe he would draw the wrong conclusion.

The idea ought to have led to a feeling of security and relief; it was curious that it did neither. But, while she was welcoming the new arrivals, David was called to the door again. And this time he appeared leading Ben Congreve, a distinctly uncertain note in his voice as he invited the stranger inside.

'Ah, Ben.' Ellie's smile faltered as she looked at him, trying to pretend her heart had not just skipped a beat and trying, really trying, not to make comparisons between the two men. They were chalk and cheese. One so kind, and... Friendly detachment was her aim, and she might just achieve it. 'I'm so pleased you could make it.'

Introductions took a moment or two, followed by her request to David that he might find a drink for Ben. They settled amiably round the fire, the buzz of conversation became general and the atmosphere of friendliness enabled her to slip away to check on how things were in the kitchen.

Why, oh, why, she asked herself as she arranged plates of chilled soup, topping each with a blob of crème fraiche and chives, did perfectly ordinary little tasks become so labour intensive the moment there were guests waiting in the other room? She put the main dish into the top oven to reheat, drained potatoes and left them to steam, then dealt with the other vegetables.

A meeting of her image in a Victorian mirror was quite by accident, but it was reassuring. The patterned skirt showed off her small waist and the intense blue of her shirt, long sleeves turned back, was good with her colouring, especially with the pink and blue scarf knotted round the throat.

The flushed look, she told herself grimly, was indicative of the long hours spent over the stove—not the image she would have chosen tonight of all nights—though why this evening was any different from a dozen others... But an unflurried image was the one she would have chosen to project. Not that it could be helped. Best to think the delicate flush was becoming; there were times when she was too pale. And tonight there was a sparkle in her eyes which she had no wish to attribute to anything out of the ordinary.

She whisked into the sitting room and moments later all her guests were round the table: David on her right, as if to establish his precedence, Clive on her other side, with Ben as far away as possible. Which had seemed a good idea at the planning stage, but now each time she raised her head they could hardly avoid eye contact.

'David, would you mind pouring the wine?' Rising, she began to collect plates, slipping them into the dishwasher as discreetly as she could before taking from the Aga the dish of chicken with tarragon, the herbed new potatoes and the vegetables, brilliant green, red and yellow. As quickly as she could she spooned the creamy chicken onto plates which were passed round. 'I'm sorry,

I forgot to say Andrew couldn't make it. He faxed me from Turkey to apologise.'

'Mmm, I *was* going to ask.' Tanya, on Ben's left, began to explain to him. 'Andrew is a neighbour. He runs an import company and travels a lot. Rather like you, Ellie. She's one of our local success stories.' Tanya, though on the wrong side of fifty, was a natural flirt and obviously found Ben well worth the effort. She wrinkled her nose at him and smiled. 'You've probably gathered that. If her business continues as it is doing then *she'll* soon be faxing us to cancel our supper parties.'

'You think there's any danger of that?' Ben, smiling, sipping his wine, let his eyes slide from Tanya to their hostess.

'No danger at all.' Ellie was unusually crisp; she had no intention of being the centre of their conversation. 'More broccoli, Liz, Ben?'

'I hope that doesn't happen.' Liz, who had been rather quiet all evening, helped herself to some carrots. 'At least, of course I hope Ellie's business will keep on growing, but not expand so much that she goes and leaves us. She's one of our main assets in this village. We can spare her for the odd flight to Hong Kong, but apart from that... Did I hear that's where you and she met?'

'Not exactly.' Again Ben was drinking and looking directly across at her, though she had already noticed he had the curious ability of dividing his attention.

'Yes, it was.' Ellie's simultaneous interjection had a curious insistence, and she had no idea what had prompted it, except that his eyes had that probing, questioning speculation, as if he might be teetering on the edge of some recollection... 'At least...' Her voice drifted as she realised everyone was waiting for her to continue but she had lost her thread.

'Well...' Ben's tone was dry. 'You were still completely jet lagged, so you may still have been in Hong Kong, but the rest of us were, I promise you, in Singapore.' A raised eyebrow challenged her to disagree, and there was a murmur of laughter round the table. 'I did, after all, go there for a very specific purpose. At Jenny's and Robert's?' He suggested, in a kindly, querying tone.

'I'm sorry.' She felt foolish and confused. 'Of course, you're right. I simply meant we met on my Hong Kong trip but in fact in Singapore.' Then, as the laughter grew louder, she smiled ruefully, shrugged at her own loss of concentration and, forgetting the posture she had decided was safe, allowed her own amusement to bubble over, her eyes sparkling at Ben over the rim of her glass.

And she was instantly aware of his appreciation, in the way his eyes grew more intense and intimate, to an extent excluding everyone else in the room, certainly making her heart go into overdrive, thundering against her ribs, sucking the breath from her body. It was quite a mind-blowing sense of euphoria, dangerous to indulge but for a few seconds impossible to resist.

And he was aware of it too, burningly conscious that simply looking at her made him feel his bones would melt with the power... Suddenly aware that the doctor, David, was asking something about his work, if he were in business, he brought himself back to the present.

'No.' He glanced at Ellie, maybe wondering how she might have described him to her neighbours. 'Not exactly. I'm a writer, you see, and went to Singapore to do research.'

'A writer?' Tanya was, if possible, even more intrigued than before. 'Interesting. And why,' she asked, echoing Ben's questioning look at Ellie, 'didn't you say a word about having met a writer?'

'I haven't really had the chance. I've barely seen you since I got back, and besides, I was by no means certain Ben would want to chat about his work. People can be touchy about these things, and might hate having questions fired from all corners.'

'I shall ignore that and dive straight in, Ben. Do tell us what you write. And, please, no translations of some obscure fourteenth-century verse for the stage.'

'No, not as bad as that.' Seeing his hostess begin to collect plates and dishes, Ben rose to help, following her to the dishwasher and placing the dirty plates at the side, where they could easily be loaded. 'No,' he went on as he walked back. 'Sixteenth and early seventeenth would be closer, and Tibetan rather than Chinese, but…'

'Don't believe him.' Grinning, Ellie handed him one of the puddings brought from the larder. 'He's much more up to date than that.' Sitting, she began to serve her guests, slicing carefully into the chocolate gâteau bought from her favourite London patisserie, spooning generous portions of bread and butter pudding for those who preferred that.

'This is my favourite of all time—the way to a man's heart,' David explained to the company at large, and in so doing, Ellie suspected, was stating his position to the stranger. 'And no one makes it quite like Ellie. Certainly it never tasted like that at school.'

'No, that's true,' his sister confirmed ruefully. 'I can never quite get it right, no matter how I try…'

'It's delicious, we know.' Tanya was clearly impatient

to hear more of the writer and less of the pudding. 'And this, too—' she forked a tiny piece of gâteau '—is sheer heaven, but I want to hear more about Ben and his writing. Do tell us exactly what you write, and is it published under your own name or...?'

'Mostly I write modern crime novels, one or two with historical themes. I have been criticised for glamorising criminals, but I think I'm reflecting life as it is. Many of our more successful villains are known more for their lifestyle than for their crimes, that and their exposure in gossip columns. Believe me, the last thing you would associate with some of the names is large-scale fraud, extortion, racketeering.'

'So, what are you saying, Ben?' Clive forestalled his wife.

Ben put down his fork and sat back in his chair, a thoughtful expression on his tanned face, 'I'm saying if I were to mention certain names you would think, incredible lifestyles, private jets, hideaway islands, the most beautiful women you could imagine. You would think influential friends, prime ministers, presidents falling over themselves...'

'Is it really so corrupt?' David sounded just a little prim and judgemental. 'I'd have thought anyone seeking public office has to choose his friends with care, to keep his hands clean—especially these days with so much media scrutiny.'

'The problem is, these men—and it's usually men—who are involved appear to have laundered, unimpeachable backgrounds. Their children have been to the best schools and universities. Money can buy almost anything you care to mention. They are surrounded by armies of clever lawyers, so you could put the whole of the FBI, Scotland Yard and the Sûreté onto them and they would come up with nothing. They have been covering their tracks for years, you see, but there eventually comes a time when they drift, sometimes quite by chance, into legitimate pursuits and get found out.'

'It sounds so…depressing.'

'It's a dirty world out there, or rather,' Ben corrected himself, smiling apologetically, 'part of it is very dark and dirty, but fortunately the vast majority is relatively clean. I guess it was always so.'

Ellie offered second helpings of the pudding, asked David to refill glasses, and saw from Ben a speculative glance which tried to work out their relationship. Then, rather perversely, she sat back in her chair, sipping her wine, savouring her sense of power as she teased her unexpected guest. 'But, Ben, Tanya did ask another question which you haven't yet answered…'

'Did I?' For a moment Tanya looked blank, then, 'Oh, yes, of course. I asked if you wrote under your own name.'

'No.' Ben smiled drily. 'I use a pseudonym. I write as Jonas Parnell.'

It was, to Ellie, a silence which was long and dramatic, but, thinking of it later, she felt she might have exaggerated. It seemed so long because she and Ben were staring at each other, she feeling guilty, abashed, and he… Well, he might have been accusing. But his expression was impossible to identify, and Tanya didn't give anyone much time for consideration—but then she never did.

'Jonas Parnell! Jonas Parnell!' She repeated the name on a note of rising incredulity. 'Clive has all of your books.' The face she turned towards her husband on the opposite side of the table was aglow with excitement. 'And that means... Clive, you know that film we watched the other night, all about piracy on the high seas—*First Sea Lord* it was called—I'm sure that was by...'

'I was about to say the same thing myself.' From time to time Clive made an effort to subdue his wife's exuberant style, and now shot her a disapproving look, on principle rather than because she had done much to displease him. He turned to Ben. 'You've struck most of us dumb, Ben—Tanya excepted. Well, nothing can accomplish that. But how amazing. And Ellie, you dark horse, how dare you keep this piece of news from your friends? You know...' again he was speaking to Ben more than to the others '...we all met last week, asked about her trip to the Far East, and she made no mention about having met you.'

'Well, I should hardly have expected her to remember.' Ellie glared across as Ben spoke. Coming from him this was a bit rich, and it was annoying that he refused to meet her eyes.

'In fact, from what she said,' Clive continued, 'she spent all her time with her nose to the grindstone, but now it appears she had time for a social life. Now why all the secrecy, Ellie? What were you hiding? If we had known we could have brought all our paperbacks with us and had them signed by the author.'

Damn you, Clive, you're becoming as garrulous as your wife. But in spite of the mean thought she felt the colour rise in her face, knew Ben Congreve was smart enough to read the guilty signals correctly, would draw heaven knew what kind of conclusion. 'I suppose if I told you I had no idea we would ever meet again, had

no idea he was even in England, you wouldn't believe
me...'

Sadly, Clive shook his head, sighed, 'I'm afraid not.
You've forfeited our trust.'

'Well...' She could produce a smile without actually
joining in the laughter. 'I shall have to appeal to Ben.
He will confirm what I have just said...' She turned a
confident face to the American, who, to her chagrin,
shook his head with apparent regret.

'I'm sorry, Ellie, I really cannot...'

'You what?' Ellie frowned, wondering for a second if
they were talking at cross purposes, and then, seeing the
grin pass over Ben's face, she felt that subtle little jolt
in the region of her diaphragm. To think she had almost
forgotten this part of his personality. One of his most
attractive characteristics had been this inclination for
light-hearted teasing; it was one of the things she had
fallen in love with.

The recollection, however tenuous, was at that moment most unwelcome. She stared, eyes shadowy with
pain, and found he was gazing back as if searching for
the solution to an elusive problem, oblivious of the continuing laughter and chatter. Only David seemed aware
of some potent underlying tensions.

David frowned as he looked, perplexed, from one to
the other. 'You cannot mean your visit *was* arranged?'
A sense of humour had never been one of David's major
strengths, it was one of the things which made it possible
for Ellie to hesitate, but still, she would not have him
think...

'Of course he doesn't mean that.' As well as all her
other feelings she was beginning to feel guilty about the
inevitable comparisons she was making between the two

men, always unfair to David, who was one of the most decent men... 'It's simply that he always enjoys stirring things up. Isn't that so, Ben?'

'If you say so.' Again that curious expression, as if he were searching his memory, trying to find an answer to some nebulous query. He came out of his reverie to smile round the table. 'And of course Ellie is perfectly right. She had no idea who was about to descend on her, I promise you. The table was set for just five people. And it was a delicious meal, Ellie, thank you for taking pity on a poor exiled Yank.'

'Exiled? Does that mean they won't let you back into the States?'

'Probably all those Mafia types waiting for him.' When David had had the last word as if by common consent they all rose from the table and went into the sitting room where, after checking on drinks, Ellie sneaked away to make the coffee. She was about to pick up the tray when she heard a step behind her and saw Ben in the doorway.

'I thought you might like some help.' He came forward, stood watching while Ellie poured water into the cafetière.

'All under control.' Best to be crisp, to convince herself she was unaffected by his presence. Not easy when he looked so striking in dark trousers, a jacket in soft caramel-coloured linen, cream shirt and striped tie. Funny to think all her memories of him were of a near naked figure, but she mustn't allow... She wrenched at her subversive thoughts while avoiding eye contact, 'If you can manage the tray, I'll bring the coffee.'

Don't. Ben Congreve had the sudden urge to say to

her. Don't treat me like your house-trained GP. He might not mind it; I certainly do.

The strength of his feelings shocked him, especially in view of his offer of help, but there was so much about this woman that puzzled him. He had made this trip not knowing what to expect, half hoping a cure might be effected, that he would find her less mysterious, less intriguing, but the reverse seemed to be the case. She was a Sphinx, a paradox, whose secrets he meant to unravel regardless of the cost. To unravel and eventually possess. But he must be patient.

'You are, Ellie,' he said, his tone mild, 'a very controlled young woman.'

His opinion was one Ellie neither expected nor appreciated, and, knowing what she did, remembering all the struggles to subdue a passionate nature, she felt wounded at his assessment. But, judging it best to take his remark as a compliment, she smiled, tried to ignore the agitated beating of her heart and shrugged lightly. 'When one is in business, I think one has to be.'

Ben reached out for the tray, his move coinciding with a move of Ellie's so their fingers brushed, producing an extraordinary little frisson as if she had been grazed by an electric charge. Taking a backward step, she struggled for composure, absurdly pleased when her voice remained steady. 'I'm sure you find that when you're writing, you have to be firm with yourself, or you would never finish.'

'Or, in my case, never start.' If he had experienced that same stabbing sensation then he wasn't showing it. He stood with the tray while she picked up the coffee pot and went ahead into the sitting room, where David, she was pleased to see, was acting host and throwing some logs onto the fire.

The rest of the evening passed pleasantly enough. All her guests gave the impression of enjoyment, and if she was quieter than usual, no one seemed to notice. But it was something of a relief to her when David had a call on his mobile and had to dash off to an emergency.

'Don't worry about Liz,' Clive was reassuring him. 'We'll see she gets home safely. I'll take her to the front door myself.'

'Thanks, Clive. I'm sorry to be breaking up your evening, love.' When Ellie went to the door with him, he leaned forward to kiss her cheek, as he always did, while she, aware of the open door of the sitting room, returned the embrace with much more fervour than usual. She went back to her other guests, reassured in some strange way by the fact that Ben could not have avoided seeing.

But that was the signal for them all to go, although Tanya showed her usual reluctance. 'They're all such country people, Ben—must be in bed by eleven. But I'm a townie, and it's not so long since I used to disco the nights away...'

'Come on, love.' Clive took her arm. 'Maybe you'll meet Ben another time and he can tell you how to write a bestseller. That's why she doesn't want to go home, Ben. She wants to pick your brains. Last week we met an artist and Tanya had this idea she might take the art world by storm. She talked of buying an easel and palette, but I'm sure a word processor, or even a scribbling pad, would be much more practical. Anyway, I can see that for the next week I shall be used as a sounding board for all kinds of plots.'

Tanya, used to being teased, smiled patiently and

sighed a little. 'You won't be saying that if I do write a book, but come on, we mustn't keep Ellie standing in the hall for ever.' And with a flurry of goodbyes the three went off.

Ellie closed the door softly, wondering with a nervous shiver how long Ben meant to stay. Wondering, too, just what her friends were making of the fact that he had shown no inclination to leave with them.

'I like your friends.' He followed her back into the sitting room, sat opposite her, stretching his long legs out towards the dying embers.

'Yes, I'm very lucky. We all get along well.'

'But you do have other friends, of your own age?'

'What has age to do with it?' Her tone showed irritation. 'One doesn't choose one's friends on the basis of age; it all develops slowly.'

'Yes, but they are all a bit older—more your parents' generation, I would have thought.'

'That's how I like my friends.' A touch of sarcasm. 'I'm sorry if you think I've been careless in my choice.'

For a longish time they simply stared at each other, she quite aware of the sparkiness in her manner and not regretting it. Then he said, 'Perhaps they were your husband's friends?'

'No, none of them knew him.' Disconcerted by his attention, she altered her position, sitting sideways on the sofa, slipping her feet out of her sandals and swinging her legs onto the seat.

'Is it painful for you to speak of him, Ellie?'

'No, it isn't painful, but it isn't something I do much. I prefer to keep certain things to myself. Remember, we spoke of this earlier, and notice I have shown no curiosity about your relationships.'

'That is supposed to please me?' His tone was of light self-mockery. 'I promise you, Ellie, even if I didn't want to answer your questions, I would be delighted that you had enough interest to ask them.'

'Really?' Smiling, yawning in a lazy, smothered little gesture, she stretched out her feet towards the fire, saw his eyes follow her moves then return to her face. Slowly she shook her head, aware of the hair floating out about her face, conscious for the first time since they'd met up of having some kind of power. 'But I have no intention of prying into your private life.'

He shrugged, dark eyes glittering in the light from the fire, and he smiled too, as if acknowledging that she was putting him down, that he didn't like it but was willing to go along with it for the time being, but then he spoke again. 'David?'

He got to his feet, strode to the window, stood for a moment, then swung round, came back to stand close before perching at the far end of the sofa, just inches from her feet. It was an effort of sheer will for her to remain as she was, apparently relaxed, at ease.

'Am I right in thinking that you and he are...?' He made a rocking movement with his hand.

'He's...a good friend.'

Ben continued to smile but his eyes had narrowed. She was sure her slight hesitation had been an irritant, and she found herself adding to what she had said without meaning to do so.

'He and Liz have been my friends since he bought the practice three years ago.'

'And he's how old? Forty, forty-five?'

'As a matter of fact I believe he's forty-seven.' Anger was growing now. This man who had caused her years of anguish was daring to disapprove. 'But, as I said, I don't think of people's ages.'

'He's too old for you.'

'I'm not sure what that means,' she lied. 'But I'm sure that whatever it means it's none of your business. Whatever my relationship with David Merriman.'

'Even if he were thirty, he would be too old for you, Ellie.' As he spoke his fingers came out, circled her instep, bringing her heart hammering into her throat, sending her emotions haywire. A series of snapshots flashed through her brain, bringing back memories of an almost unbearable sweetness.

Holding her eyes wide, she tried to dislodge from her mind that last night on the island when they had skinny-dipped from the boat, rejoicing in the freedom, in the dreamy magic of the tropical night, in the sheer ecstatic joy of life and love. But the scenes kept clicking. She was seeing, feeling again, the seemingly random tracing of his fingers across her skin, that powerful jolt as they closed round her foot, the casual brush of skin against tender skin making it impossible for her to withdraw from his sensuous, stroking touch. As it was now.

But move she must. If she were to delay an instant longer there was no saying... 'So...' A superhuman effort and she was levering herself upright, detaching herself, swinging her legs onto the floor, her feet into her shoes and standing, more than a little relieved that her legs were capable of supporting her. She spent a moment adjusting the wide belt about her slender waist. 'So you don't approve of my friendship with David.' Now she was calm enough to look at him she noted a glitter of something like anger in the dark eyes, but she was unmoved. 'I shall *try* to remember.' And she was rather pleased with her dismissive tone.

'And now you want to go to bed?' Lazily, he unwound himself from his perch on the end of the sofa and stood, eyes fixed disconcertingly on her mouth.

'It's been a long day, and I confess, I'm tired.'

'Sure.' He was disarmingly amiable. 'And it was a delicious meal, Ellie. You're really a very good cook.'

She was glad she could be honest in the face of so much deception. 'Most of it was prepared by Wendy before she took Charlie off. The only part I had a hand in was that silly pudding.' Ridiculous to be speaking to him of bread and butter pudding, and in spite of herself she smiled, shook her head so the titian hair flew about her like a mane aglow with energy. 'English men and their nursery puddings.' There was a tremble in her voice as she saw his eyes follow the movement of her hair, a weakness which increased when he walked forward, took her hand and brushed against it once or twice with his thumb.

'Don't.' She snatched at her hand, glaring up at him. 'Please don't touch me.'

'Honey.' How she remembered that endearment, uttered in that melting, tender way designed to convince a woman…to weaken and seduce. 'If you don't want me to touch you then, of course, I shan't come close, but…I wasn't threatening.' He held up his hands in a gesture of innocence. 'But I wonder what makes you so…so nervy.'

'Nothing.' She rubbed the palms of her hands down over her arms. 'Nothing at all. In fact, I'm not a nervy person.' All at once her anger against him dissolved. 'I suppose I'm just tired.'

'OK. That figures.' His smile was guarded. 'And I'm sorry if I upset you in any way; it was the last thing in my mind if I did. I'm still kinda hoping you'll meet me before I go back…'

'I don't think so, do you?' Such an effort to smile when she was overwhelmed with desolation. If they truly were meeting for the last time… Maybe she had played it all wrong. If she had been less abrasive, they might have exchanged a farewell kiss. The very thought of his mouth against hers, however chastely… She stifled a groan. She had denied herself that torture, for it wouldn't have been enough, not nearly enough, so it was for the best. 'Besides, I'm really under pressure right now—so many designs to be vetted before they go off to Hong Kong, and…'

'Well, I can see you've made up your mind.' Raising a hand to touch her cheek, he grimaced and dropped it before there was contact. 'I shall let you have your way for the time being, but don't think I've given up, Ellie Osborne.' His eyes grew still more searching, more intense, as if he were trying to uncover some elusive paradox. 'When I make up my mind I'm a very determined man, and I made up my mind about you the first time I saw you.'

'Oh?' An indrawn breath, panic instantly controlled.

'Mmm.' Still he was puzzled, sensing her alarm, unable to decode it. 'On Robert Van Tieg's balcony.'

'Ah—' a sigh '—I see.'

'You do?' It was a very reflective tone, and for a further endless moment he stared, unaware, or so it seemed, of the agitated rise and fall of her breast beneath the thin silk shirt. 'But some time ago you told me you were tired,' he said, returning from his reverie. 'So, I'll say goodnight, Ellie. Sleep well.' And she was alone.

For a long time she stood there, staring at the closed door, before returning to the sitting room where she fixed the guard in front of the fireplace, sank onto the sofa to watch the dying embers through the fine mesh. Hardly aware of what she was doing, she leaned forward, touched the place on her instep where his fingers had circled the fragile bones. Long, long ago that gesture had been so arousing, and guess what... Nothing had changed.

The very admission set off the alarm bells in her brain, and she was running up the curving staircase, into her bedroom, slamming the door behind her as if two inches of English oak could offer any protection from her inner demons.

And even when she was in bed, staring into the darkness, there was no sense of security, none of the peace she longed for. All he had done, it seemed, was to come back into her life and then to leave. To leave her more abandoned and desolate than she had ever been before.

CHAPTER FIVE

AMAZING. When Ellie woke in the stillness of the autumn morning, she stretched luxuriously, her mind blank, untroubled with all the trauma of the previous night which ought, by all the rules, to have kept her awake into the early hours. But that hadn't happened, blessedly. Soon after she had pulled the duvet over her head she had fallen into a deep, refreshing sleep, her dread of a spell of futile nostalgia unrealised.

Only when she got up, showered and dressed in a pair of burgundy tartan trousers, pulled on a cream silk polo, only then did she acknowledge the growling pain in the middle of her diaphragm. For a time it pleased her to pretend it was down to the surfeit of rich foods, more wine than she was used to, but deep down she had little doubt about the real reason.

But, in the meantime, she had lots of tidying up to do. Over the years she had found that intense activity was the surest balm for pain and unhappiness. With her chin set, she began to unload the dishwasher.

Back in the village inn, Ben Congreve straightened his tie, thinking, as he smiled ruefully at his reflection, that he was acting like a youngster about to have his first date. Impossible to understand what there was about this woman, except... Another thought was triggered, pain as he remembered his father's sudden death last year and the subsequent revelation, but maybe the Congreve men were particularly vulnerable where English women were concerned.

Of course he didn't really believe that. He had met a number, had even dated one or two since his divorce, but there had been nothing different or special about them, nothing to make the pulses race as Ellie Osborne was capable of doing without even trying. Perhaps it was this elusive air of mystery about her which...

Oh, what the hell. Impatiently he turned away from the mirror. He had never been the kind of guy who gave up when the going got rough, as it had once or twice in his otherwise privileged existence, and he wasn't going to do so now. Not when he had this powerful gut feeling that his whole future happiness was in the balance. But life had taught him to be patient, and he sensed that if he were to rush in like an impetuous youngster...

No, he was enjoying, *almost* enjoying the chase—although in a perverse sort of way. And he would not give it up. Not until he saw the Merriman wedding ring on her finger. And that was something he was determined would never happen.

By eleven o'clock Ellie had dealt with her immediate chores, was sitting at the kitchen table taking a ten-minute break while she drank a cup of coffee and glanced at the Sunday papers. She sighed wearily at the intrusive sound of the door knocker. She hoped it wasn't David. He was so meticulous with his thank-you notes, so determined to be first, though these days most people used the telephone.

'D—' His name died on her lips, was replaced by something very like a throb of pleasure when she threw back the door and found Ben Congreve, a huge bunch of flowers in his hand, looking almost foolishly embarrassed.

'Ellie.' He held out the bouquet, and it was impossible, when she had taken them, for her to refrain from burying her face in the deliciously scented arrangement of old-fashioned cream roses, lily of the valley and delicate ferns. 'I truly apologise for troubling you...'

'That's all right.' When she looked up her cheeks were pink, her eyes glowed, and she didn't trouble to deny that her heart had lifted on seeing him. It would be cruel to suggest it was down to relief that he wasn't David, but... 'Do come in.' She led the way into the kitchen, put the flowers down and turned to fill a glass jug with water. 'These are gorgeous, but where on earth...? They can't have come from the Red Cow.'

'No, I had them sent down from London...'

'Sent down?' Incredulity at such an extravagant gesture. 'From London? I can't believe that.'

'True, nevertheless. I called my London hotel—they have an in-house florist—and I asked them to put some on the early train, which they did. In fact, I asked for a posy—I had the idea you might think this slightly ostentatious. But anyway, hey presto...' He grinned boyishly, as if pleased with his resourcefulness.

'What it is to have...' her voice choked on the word 'charm', which she had been about to use '...contacts,' she finished lamely. 'But they are lovely. Luxurious, I would say, not ostentatious.'

He strolled across to the Aga and stood, one hand leaning against the blue-tiled surround, rangy and apparently relaxed, which she most certainly was not, thought Ellie with a flash of indignation. 'As I said, they are really an apology for troubling you again. I suppose you could have done with a day to yourself after all yesterday's preparations, but I had to come, you see. I think I must have left something here last night.'

'Oh?' Ellie frowned. 'I don't think so. At least, I haven't noticed…'

'Well, you wouldn't.' Straightening up, he went to the door. 'Do you mind if I look?' And, when she nodded, he walked through to the sitting room, Ellie a step behind, crossed to a table in the far corner close to where he had been sitting, picked something up and turned, brandishing a small book. 'Here it is. Thank you, Ellie, I should be lost without my list of telephone numbers.'

He pushed it into the pocket of his grey trousers. 'I was taking down Tanya's number—at her insistence, I might add. She wants me to give a talk to some women's group—is it raising money for a children's hospice?'

'Mmm. Sounds like one of Tanya's projects.'

'Quite by chance I told her I would be back in England before the end of the year and she popped that one out at me. I didn't stand a chance.'

'No, most people don't. But I'm glad you found it.'

'Well, now I have, I'd better go…'

'Have you time for a coffee?' Why on earth…? Even as she heard the words it was difficult for Ellie to believe she was doing this. It was simply… Oh, she had no idea what it was, but before she had time to withdraw they were back in the kitchen and she was pouring hot water onto coffee grounds, trying to banish the certainty that she was being incredibly foolish, making herself vulnerable, and besides…she had a mountain of work…

'Another reason for coming was that I'm still hoping we might get together one more time before I have to fly back to the States…'

'Oh, I don't think I can make it.' Thank goodness. A bit of sense at last. And she was able to produce a mildly regretful smile as she poured the coffee into a mug. 'Some other time, perhaps.' She made an attempt to soften the refusal, though she determined to be firm. 'But I might come to the talk you plan to give for Tanya's ladies.'

'That—' he leaned across the table, spoke with barely suppressed passion '—is *not* what I had in mind.' For a long time he glared, then wrenched his attention away, stirring sugar into his black coffee with the concentration of a medieval alchemist, glaring again as he raised the cup to his mouth. 'It's a *date* I'm suggesting after all.' The mug hit the table with a bump which spilled some of the liquid onto the wood. 'Not—*not* an invitation to hear me spout banalities about writing bestsellers, which is, I gather, what Tanya has in mind.'

Automatically Ellie reached out for a damp cloth and, without hurrying, mopped the puddle of coffee, returning his stare and apparently unmoved by his anger. But it gave her an inward buzz that at last *he* was showing some signs of frustration. It was no more than he deserved after all. And there was the additional frisson of satisfaction that this time she was the one wielding the hatchet and, by heaven, she meant to keep on doing just that.

'A date,' he went on in a more considered tone, 'with your daughter as chaperone, if you insist. If it will make things easier for you.'

At that, she felt a stab of sheer bloody-minded anger. It was as if he were disowning his only child. Only child? But how would she ever know that? How would *he* know, since his behaviour was so careless, so cavalier? Gritting her teeth in an attempt to control her emotions, she returned his gaze calmly. She rose with the intention of fetching a tin of biscuits by way of diversion. 'It's flattering that you want to take me out. Of course it is.' She was well aware her ironic tone was conveying the opposite message. 'But I don't go out much at nights...' About to open a cupboard, she found it slammed shut as he came up behind her. Slammed shut by the simple course of placing his hand on the door and leaning.

'For God's sake! At least have the courage to speak the truth. That I can accept, even if it isn't what I want to hear. Evasions are something else. Last night when you were in the kitchen, your doctor friend regaled us with the story of your trip to London to a concert—one in a series, I believe, so don't tell me you don't go out at night, Ellie.'

This slightly aggressive, sharply spoken man was one she did not recognise. He brought to her spine a little shiver of nervous excitement.

'I suppose Charlie was dumped with...with what's-her-name for the night? And when you came back with David—' his scorn for the man was something he did not trouble to hide '—did you share your bed with him?'

'How dare you?' Brilliant eyes stared up at him as she struggled to control the lacerating pain, but it wasn't the implication of an affair with David which was so wounding—that could easily come later—right now it was his implication that she dumped her child whenever it suited her. So rich, coming from a man who presumably dumped his lovers all over the world and conveniently forgot about them. While she... Fury added to her emotions. *She* had had the full burden of pregnancy, lonely and neglected.

At least—her thoughts were becoming jumbled—she would have had without the lucky chance of meeting Greg Osborne, of allowing herself to be persuaded into marriage so she could have a home. 'You are contemptible.' Anger made her lips curl in undisguised scorn; it was either that or howling with misery, which was something her pride would never allow.

'Do you know...?' Ben put his hands on her shoulders, anger against her rising in him like a tidal bore. But the almost irresistible desire to shake her was one he forced himself to control, so at once he released her, then reached out to steady her. Violence towards women was something he had never understood...and every urge in his body was to protect this woman. To possess and protect, he amended, the second almost as powerful as the first. He thrust his hands into the pockets of his trousers. 'You are the most aggravating woman I have met in a very long time.'

'So, the other women in your life are just mildly aggravating?' Ellie spoke with deliberate coldness. 'Compared with me, that is.' She raised a sarcastic eyebrow.

Ben stood for a moment, considering. What would be the point in telling her that his outburst of a moment earlier had been a reaction to a surge of insane, murderous jealousy, that there had been a split second when he had thought of her sharing her bed with...? One or two deep breaths and he had himself under control again.

'I have offended you and I'm sorry, Ellie. It was the last thing I had in mind when I came over. As you have told me before, I have no right to ask anything about your private life.' He was doing this rather well, he thought with slightly bitter amusement, but penitence seemed the wisest choice in the circumstances. 'If you sleep with the…with David,' he amended tactfully, 'it's your business entirely, yours and his, and I have no right to comment.'

'It wasn't that.' She was stonily unforgiving, 'I don't give a tuppenny damn for your opinion of David, or any other man I care to sleep with.' Let him make what he would out of that. She had her feelings well under control now, and there was no need to avoid lashing out at him. 'It was…' Her voice trembled.

'Tell me.'

'Damn you, why did you have to imply I dumped Charlie simply to enjoy a night out? Have you any idea of the guilt I feel when I have to leave her? All working mothers are tormented when they have to trust others with their babies, and you have to turn the knife…'

Resisting the impulse to close in, to beat her fists against his chest, she faced him defiantly. 'People like you, people born with silver spoons, have no idea what it's like to have to support themselves and their family in something like comfort. What would you know about all the juggling of time and attention? Why is it that working mothers *dump* their children but no one uses that word about fathers…?'

'Hey.' Now he trusted himself to put his hands on her shoulders and give her a tiny friendly shake. 'Hey. I'm sure you're a great mother. I had no intention of implying anything else. It was simply for a moment I wanted to do away with your revered GP.'

'And the times you miss out on the school concert because of a vital rushed order, the birthdays when you give less than your full attention because you expect the bailiffs to call and take away your means...'

'OK.' He held up his hands in a gesture of surrender, not wholly serious because he was smiling. 'OK. I'm convinced. It's a hard life and I know you've done spectacularly well. I know because of the way you speak of your daughter, how your eyes soften. I *know* from what Jenny told me, and—'

'Jenny?' She snatched at the name, looked at him accusingly, eyes fiery and passionate as ever. 'What has Jenny been saying about me? I *do* wish my friends didn't have this compulsion to gossip. It isn't—'

'Come *on*, Ellie, we all talk about our friends. And from what I've heard, all yours are devoted to you.'

'Well...' Realising she was losing it, she struggled for calm.

'And once again I have to tell you Jenny volunteered nothing. She knew I was interested in you—attracted, if you want the truth—and since she knows you are single, as I am, she may have thought she was doing us a favour. Certainly she was doing me one, and since she knows I'm not some mad kind of stalker...'

'She *knows* I'm not in the market for a serious relationship.'

'Who said anything about a serious relationship? You sound more like a Victorian father than a modern jet-setting career woman. And if it comes to that, *I'm* not in search of a serious relationship. I've learned enough about those to be wary, but it doesn't put me off wanting to date a woman who attracts me—more than that, who fascinates me.' He gazed down, a tiny frown pulling his eyebrows together. 'Only I begin to wonder about your relationship with your husband. Was it so blissful no other man could compete, or…so dire it put you off mating for evermore?'

Ellie gave a little shiver, rejecting any thought of debating that point with him, instead turning away to do something at the sink. 'You're right, of course. I'm getting things out of perspective. It's simply that I've fallen out of the habit of dating, lost the knack somehow, and…'

'And David offers an opportunity which is unthreatening?'

'I was about to say, it's something I haven't particularly missed, and perhaps even an exercise which offers as much pain as pleasure.'

'Well…' he considered. 'That's true of so many things in life, but it's no reason to fear them.'

'Fear?' She countered indignantly. 'I didn't say I feared it, simply that I have learned not to miss it, to prefer the freedom to go my own way without the needless complications which intense relationships inevitably involve, to decide things which suit us with no reference to anyone else.'

'Mmm. Who has hurt you so much, Ellie, that you are wary of any kind of commitment?'

For a moment the pain was so raw she was robbed of the power of speech, unable to do more than stare at him, the architect of so much that had gone wrong. Never had she imagined a scene in which this man would pose this particular question.

And Ben Congreve, staring back into those wonderfully translucent eyes, felt her pain as if it were his own. That the question should be so hard for her to answer meant he was ashamed of having asked it. And yet the attraction he felt for her was so insistent, so powerful, so much more profound than anything that had come his way before, and it was touched by something deeper, an elusive something he could not quite put a finger on. It wasn't simply her striking looks—most men would have been attracted to those eyes, fascinated by that yearning tender mouth. She was a woman made to be loved. And by him, Ben Congreve. Since he had met her he seemed to have been struggling with that obscure region of his memory...

Her voice broke in. 'I think your problem is that you are so unused to being turned down you have to find some reason, invent one if necessary, to salve your pride.'

She might be right at that, Ben decided, though not in the way she meant. He shrugged lightly. 'That is your theory, Ellie, and I'm sorry to disagree with you. I have—hard though it is to believe—been turned down before now, and my pride wasn't damaged in the least.'

This was sufficiently unlikely for her merely to raise a sceptical eyebrow, but at the same time, suspecting that her resistance was being eroded, oh, so gradually, she made to move away from him, only to find her way blocked.

And there was no fight, no resistance left, when, with a combination of disarming gentleness and total determination, he tipped her chin so they were looking inescapably at each other. A thumb brushed her mouth in that well-remembered gesture, her lips parted involuntarily as her breathing increased, and it would have been difficult for him to miss the rapid rise and fall of her breast so close to his. Then his hand was on her ribcage, just below the breast, where he could be in little doubt of her reaction.

'You see…' He spoke so softly it was almost a whisper, so intimate, so… 'I feel exactly the same.' And his mouth closed on hers.

The possibility of opposition was long since gone. Having struggled so long against surrender, she felt a sense of release as she allowed herself this one kiss. But she had forgotten. For all the endless dreams, she had forgotten how beguiling it could be, this first step along a path, especially when heart, emotions, her very being were so involved. Her legs grew weak, and but for the powerful arm about her waist she might have sunk to the ground.

And then, denying him the monopoly of initiative, she responded. How could it be otherwise when all her senses were engaged, were yearning for a closer, a more intimate contact? She linked her fingers through his hair, held his mouth against hers and gave herself up to the torment of the moment, knowing it could not last.

And then, just in the nick of time—or so she told herself later with a touch of bitterness—to save her from herself, there were sounds from outside. The front door was pushed open, her daughter's laugh rang out as she ran across the hall and into the kitchen.

Charlie. She stopped suddenly in the doorway, stilled in her tracks by the sight of her mother and a strange man so close. 'Mummy.' She took a few steps, hesitated, a tall child for her six years, dressed in dark cords and pale blue sweatshirt, a patterned scarf wound casually at the throat. 'Mummy.' Surprise at the stranger had dimmed her natural enthusiasm, creating the shyness she showed with men she did not know.

Her height came from both parents, Ellie realised with a pang, but the rich auburn hair had, in her daughter, been tempered to a dark leaf-brown with a hint of chestnut in certain lights, and today it was braided from the crown in her current favourite style. Her eyes were striking, expressive like her mother's. No hint there—in fact, nothing which could give a clue to Ben.

So, as the first panic began to subside, the mother was able to summon a smile, to take a few steps, to crouch down beside the child and exchange greetings. Then to turn enquiringly towards the door as Wendy, looking slightly less calm and assured than was usual, followed her into the kitchen.

'I'm so sorry, Ellie, I had to bring her back. You see, Linda—I told you she was staying with us this weekend—well, she just arrived and she's showing spots. I took her to see David and he's almost sure she has chickenpox, and since I knew you wouldn't want Charlie to go down with that over half-term, I thought the only thing I could do would be to bring her back home and hope it isn't already too late.'

'Oh, poor Linda.' Ellie rose slowly. 'And of course you did the only thing bringing her home, chickenpox is the last thing we want.' She spoke to her daughter again, 'You don't want to be stuck in bed all week, do you, Charlie?'

'No, I don't want to miss my holidays.' And then, with the smile that could charm in spite of two missing front teeth, she looked up at Ben. 'Who are you? Are you a friend of Mummy's?'

There was a second's silence while all kinds of replies echoed in Ellie's brain, and the one she heard most clearly was the one she could never use. This is your father, Charlie. His name is Ben Congreve and he has neither known nor cared for us all these years. It would have been the perfect way to settle the old bitter score.

CHAPTER SIX

WHAT Ellie did was smile with all the calm she could summon, open her mouth and speak with determined confidence, hoping her voice would not break. 'This is Ben Congreve; he's visiting from the United States. Ben, this is my daughter, Charlie, whom you've heard about, and Wendy—' she turned round '—don't stand in the doorway. This is Wendy Cummings, who has been my right-hand woman since Charlie was small. She looks after the house, does the cooking and, most important of all, she cares for Charlie when I'm away. It doesn't seem to matter when I want to...' Inclined to use the word 'dump', she changed it for her daughter's sake, but a glance confirmed that he understood. 'When I want to call on her services, she never lets me down. I simply could not function without her.'

Wendy blushed when Ben shook her hand, then in a rush went on to explain that her niece's visit, planned to coincide with half-term and to provide Charlie with companionship, looked like being a disaster. All the plans they had made for seaside visits, for picnics and anything else the girls fancied, would be thwarted.

'That can't be helped, Wendy. I just hope Linda isn't feeling too bad.'

'Well, as I say, it's disappointing for the girls, but we'll make up for it later. Now, I'll have to get home, Ellie. Bye, Charlie, keep thinking of something special for later. Nice to meet you, Mr Congreve.' And with that she was gone; they heard her car drive off.

'So, Charlie...' By this time Ben was squatting down, his head level with her. 'Half-term? Does that mean...?'

'It means school is closed for a whole week and now I shall have nothing to do.' She gave a pitiful sigh which had her mother frowning in reproof.

'When I came up your drive this morning, I saw a pony in the field.' Ben straightened up. 'Is he yours?'

'Yes, that's Flossie, but she's a lady.'

'Well, what about taking me down to introduce me? I'm quite keen on horses myself. If your mummy says it's all right.' He turned and decided to ignore Ellie's cynically raised eyebrow.

'Mum won't mind. Come on, then.' She took his hand and pulled him to the door.

'Is it all right, Ellie?'

She pursed her lips, shrugged helplessly, turning away so her expression was hidden. But when they had gone, she watched the two figures strolling down the drive, apparently engaged in conversation, Charlie with one hand thrust into the front pocket of her trousers. Ellie made no attempt to stifle the sobs which rose in her throat.

It was several minutes before she could regain control, then she ran upstairs, splashed her face with cool water, and, with determination, went back down and began, rather aimlessly, to tidy a kitchen drawer.

As far as getting on with some serious work was concerned, she'd better forget it. Even when—*if* might be more apt, in view of his tenacity—*if* Ben Congreve got the message that he was overstaying his welcome, Ellie knew today would be written off, that even later she would be too emotionally drained to cope with anything that required her concentration.

And when it came to picking up vibes, Ben Congreve chose on this occasion to be deliberately obtuse, which was how, an hour or two later, he found himself sitting in the Red Cow eating Sunday lunch with Ellie and her daughter. He felt a sense of smug amusement at the way he had out-manoeuvred her, and was by no means unaware of the speculative glances he was arousing with the locals. He felt amused pleasure, too, in seeing Charlie's pure delight as she contemplated an enormous ice cream confection, the glass so tall she could barely see over it.

But for Ellie it had been disconcerting to see Charlie respond so easily, open up before Ben's gentle teasing, to watch the coquettish tilt to her head, the sideways glance, the repressive tightening of her lips when she tried not to laugh—all the delicious feminine traits which she herself had long eschewed and which Ben was so obviously lapping up. He was a persuasive devil, always had been, and she had to be on guard against the shared amusement which his glances invited.

But at the same time there was an ache, an additional ache, she reminded herself, an anxiety felt for the first time in ages as she faced the fact that her daughter might be deprived through having no male living with the family. Remembering her own close relationship with her father, a special closeness stretching back to her very earliest memories, she knew it was something precious. That was why her attempted deceit had been so hard, why her subsequent confession had been such a release. And he had forgiven, as always. She sighed deeply, then became aware of her daughter plaintively repeating her name.

'You were miles away, Mummy.'

'I'm sorry, I was thinking.' Deliberately she avoided looking at the man opposite.

Now it was Charlie's turn to sigh, patiently. 'I was telling Ben—' a flutter of long lashes '—that my granny lives in Australia and we went out on a plane to visit her.'

The deep flush that stained Ellie's cheeks was inexplicable. She was remembering that Sydney telephone number, her sole contact with Ben Congreve, and the long hopeless wait for the call that never was. With an effort, she smiled vaguely, sensed rather than saw that he was frowning.

'That's right, darling. And it was the first time you had seen your granny, wasn't it?'

'Yes, I was four years old before she saw me, and she cried when we reached her house. But that was because Grandpa had just died.'

'Ah, well,' Ben spoke quietly, 'that would make her cry. It's always sad when someone dies.'

'Yes, we were all sad. Mummy cried too.' Of course she had, how could it have been otherwise when she had wounded them so much?

When Charlie had reapplied herself to her ice cream, Ben's voice, soft, slow, thoughtful, demanded Ellie's attention. 'Your parents live in Australia? And yet I could have sworn you were English.'

'I *am* English.' With false calm she looked at him, but with an almost detached interest, searching for some clue in his expression. This, after all, was the very background she had outlined when they first met. 'But I was taken to Australia as a teenager. My mother has MS and the climate suited her so much better, they decided to stay on.'

'My grandpa was Sir William Tenby.' Carefully, Charlie wiped off her ice cream moustache with a large napkin.

'Was he indeed? Sounds like an important man.'

Dear God! Not the least sign of recognition. Furiously Ellie stared across. Surely a name like that would spark *some* reaction? But what was she expecting? That his head should jerk round, eyes widen with joy and that he would claim her as his long-lost love? Dream on! Suddenly Ellie realised he was looking at her, the raised eyebrows obviously querying something in her expression, and it was useful when Charlie, spotting a friend, caused a diversion.

'Mummy, I can see Pippa over there. May I go and speak to her, please?'

'You've finished with that ice cream?'

'Yes, I'm sorry about that last little bit, but I've almost finished it.' They watched her hurry across to join her friend as Pippa's mother waved. Ellie allowed her eyes to rest curiously on Ben for a moment.

'She's a great kid, Ellie.' Ben's attention was still focused on the small, animated figure now deep in a confidential debate. 'You've done a brilliant job with her.' Ellie smiled briefly before he went on. 'And I'm sorry about your father. I suppose I imagined supportive parents nearby.'

'No, that would have been marvellous but...' The pain of her father's sudden death stabbed as powerfully as if it had happened last week. 'I...I told you of my mother's illness...no one could have guessed he'd be the first to go. He was formidably healthy, played tennis and squash, sailed when he had the time.' A glance towards him revealed nothing. 'But he just had a heart attack and died before help could reach him. For a time I thought my mother wouldn't get over it, but now it's amazing; we speak every week on the telephone. She's beginning to cope, but she was so used to him doing everything he could to make things easy.'

'Well, I imagine being left alone is hard for anyone, and with MS... But now you say she is managing?'

'At first I was afraid she might have to go into a nursing home, something she absolutely dreaded, but we've arranged for a series of kind people to look after her and she seems to do fairly well. In fact, she's managing so well I begin to wonder if Dad's kindness was in some way a handicap. Could it have been that through doing so much he discouraged her from doing things for herself?'

'Well, one does hear of such things.' His hand came out, touched hers briefly, was gone before she could remember and snatch hers away. 'But it's hard for you, being so far away from your mother.'

'There was a time when I almost threw everything up and moved back to Sydney with Charlie, but the business was just beginning to make real progress and Mother insisted I should hang on. My long-term plan is to move back there. Apart from anything else—' She stopped, reluctant to share her fears with him.

'Apart from anything else...?' He insisted.

No reason to avoid speaking her mind, especially when he would not make the connections. 'I was going to say, we have no family here and Charlie deserves to have contact with her relatives. Blood is thicker than water after all.'

'Certainly a child's relationship with a grandparent can be very close; I do know that.'

'Mummy, Mummy.' Charlie came hurtling back. 'I've asked Pippa to tea but her mummy says I must ask you first. Please say yes. She's got to go to visit her auntie in hospital when they've finished lunch, but her mummy says they will drop her off at our house.' ·

'Yes, that's all right. Go and tell her we'll expect to see her later.' Ellie pushed back her chair. 'And I think we should show Ben the duck pond before we walk back across the fields.'

In the glorious autumn afternoon the village was at its best, trees blazing with gold and rust in the warm sun, a light breeze ruffling the surface of the pond as they strolled across the green. While they sat watching, Charlie fed the ducks with some stale bread provided by the pub and Ellie, affected by their earlier discussion, was filled with melancholy. This, *this* was how life ought to be: two parents out with their child on a Sunday afternoon. And yet this was most likely the first and last time for Charlie…

So absorbed was she in her nostalgia she didn't notice Ben had his arm along the back of her seat, not till his hand touched her shoulder and she started.

'You look sad, Ellie.'

'No.' A determinedly bright smile. 'No, I'm not. And I enjoyed my lunch, despite my reluctance to come. Charlie certainly did, even if the knickerbocker glory defeated her.'

'I was nervous for her when I saw it. On top of all that roast beef and Yorkshire pudding.'

'Her appetite has never been what you could call delicate.'

'She's desperately disappointed that she's not going to have Linda's company over the vacation. She was telling me of all they planned to do, and…'

'Well, it's a pity, but she'll simply have to get over it. We all have to face disappointments in life; it's something we ought to get used to.' Ellie resisted the temptation to glare accusingly while she made her statement, but still a trace of bitterness showed through. 'It'll be good practice for the future.'

'I just can't believe you mean that. She's only six years old, for heaven's sake.'

'*Can't* you believe me?' Conscience, but only on her daughter's behalf, made her flare at him. 'But then, maybe you haven't had the experience life holds for many of us. It's pretty obvious you've had a privileged existence.'

'Now…I wonder what makes you so sure of that.' Again his curiosity was aroused by her attack, and the dark eyes snapped into a more searching, analytical mode. 'But, yes, as it happens, I have had a whole lot of breaks—though there have been pretty rough times as well.' She guessed he was referring to the break-up of his marriage. 'But I agree.' And though his tone was mild she was acutely aware of his probing interest. 'Compared with most people, I've had many of the good things in life.'

'Yes, I'm sorry. I ought not to blame…' aware of the risk of a blunder, she hesitated '…anyone else.'

'Blame me if it would help.' A suspicious sideways glance from Ellie detected no hidden meaning. 'But we were talking about Charlie's disappointment and I was about to make a suggestion.' Rightly interpreting her defensive look, he held up a hand and grinned. 'OK. OK. I promise, I shan't steamroller you; the decision will be entirely yours. If you give it the thumbs-down then that will be the end of the matter and not a word to you know who. Promise!'

'*You?* Promise?' The words were a shock. She'd not meant to voice them, they were meant as an inward relief valve to show exactly what she thought his promises were worth. Now she stopped, appalled, but then a tiny laugh came to her aid. 'It seems to me you've been promising not to harry me since we first met.'

'Well…' He was wary, on guard, the dark eyes intent as a panther's. 'Next week I must go to Paris. A publisher's shindig—you know the kind of thing—and it just occurred to me, what do you say to you and Charlie coming with me?' Ignoring her immediate negative murmur, he went on, 'We could travel through the tunnel. Have you done that yet?' Unable to think, she moved her head again. 'Well, I must do it, and I'd love it if you and Charlie could be with me. We could stay for a few days and go to Disneyland. I'm sure it would make up for her disappointment over Linda.'

By this time Ellie had recovered her powers of speech, was able to produce a less forced smile as she shook her head with a pretence of regret. 'You're right, of course, it would be the perfect consolation, but it's out of the question. I have a dozen reasons why I cannot possibly be away from my desk next week.'

'If you were ill, you'd have no choice.'

'No.' Her smile was growing strained. 'But I'm not ill.'

'Don't you have a deputy who can hold the fort?'

'No,' she said tartly. 'I have never had enough disposable income for that.'

'I still think it's a great idea.'

'Yes, well, I'm sure you can find any number of women who would just love to accompany you.'

Her sarcasm angered him way beyond her intention. He seized her wrist in a tight grasp, compelling her full attention, and though he spoke quietly there was a great deal of power and anger there. 'If I wanted any other woman I should not have invited you. Believe me.' And his voice throbbed with emotion.

'You are hurting me.' Anger glittered, and she spoke through clenched teeth, reluctant to admit that she was roused by his menace. But he instantly released her and she rose, crossed to where Charlie was watching a boy fishing for guppies.

Ben Congreve sat for a moment, his mind a maelstrom of black thoughts. Damn and blast the woman, and damn and blast himself. He wouldn't allow one of his fictional characters to behave like this, and yet... She was so damned irrational; that was the problem. Once or twice he had even imagined he was being accused—collective guilt of the male sex, he supposed. So what was new? And all he was doing was trying to arrange a treat for Charlie, for God's sake. Well, not *quite* all, he admitted with a wry grin, and he got up and went over to join them at the water's edge, his anger ebbing quickly.

Even now, with Charlie swinging along between them, the living link as it were, laughing at something Ben had said, some remark Ellie had missed and from which she was excluded, it was clear to Ellie they were getting on very well together. There was something close to adoration in the way the child looked up at him. The way she asked in that voice of breathless flattery if he would tell her another story about his time in Canada, when he was a boy and spent holidays there with his grandparents.

This time she did listen, and it was a saga starting among the Inuit people up on Hudson Bay and finishing at Tierra del Fuego by way of the Solomon Islands, with a limitless number of midnight dashes in emergency situations. It was so ridiculous, so amusing, that even she could not preserve her distant manner, and when they reached home and she was rummaging for the door-key she was still laughing. 'I'm surprised you're not writing children's books. Ever thought of it?' She led the way inside.

'No.' He stood in the middle of the hall, looking at her. 'But I might do some time.' His voice was slow, speculative, perhaps reminding her of her abrasive manner, and she coloured up, hating the idea that he might be disappointed in her. He had no right to be. So she turned aside, suggesting to Charlie that she run upstairs and tidy her room before Pippa arrived.

'Oh, Mummy.' Charlie, also disapproving, frowned with a look of appeal to Ben. 'I can do that later.'

'Why not do it now, honey?' Ben's voice was mild. 'And then it will be over and done with.' And, obedient as a well-trained puppy, Charlie murmured agreement and skipped upstairs, as if tidying her room was the one thing in the world she longed to do.

'Little monkey.' Ellie was exasperated, and perhaps a touch of jealousy came into it too. 'She was quite pre-pared to argue with me.'

'It's par for the course. My sister's kids are the same. In fact...' he paused, pensive '...something about her reminds me so much…' Ellie froze, heart hammering wildly, but then he went on in an amused tone. 'It's the novelty of someone new and it wears off pretty quickly.'

Ah, yes. Ellie released her breath. His sister Amy. From time to time over the years she had wondered, but this was her first chance to find out. 'You have a sister?' She knew Amy had been pregnant when they were on the Windwards…

'Yes, her name is Amy and she married Rod, who ranches in Montana. Their son Blake is seven and Jess is four. I don't see as much of them as I'd like, but it's great when I do. I find the same thing with them for the first day or two. It's ''Yes, Uncle Ben'' and they jump to it, but that wears off and life goes back to normal. If I were to see more of Charlie I'm afraid it would be the same old story.'

'Yes, I suppose…' Ellie barely heard the last few words, she was too engaged with the idea—not a new one—that Charlie had relatives out there: two cousins and an aunt. The only cousins she was likely to have in this life. It stabbed her to the heart that her daughter would never know them. In the past another thought had tormented her, that there might be half-brothers, half-sisters, but that, it seemed, had been avoided. But she felt raw and vulnerable and neglected, which was most likely why she reacted so sharply when Ben came back to the subject of Paris.

'Despite what you said, Ellie, I haven't given up hope of persuading you to come to Paris…'

'Well—' her fine eyes flashed dangerously and she felt a frisson of fear at her own weakness '—I think it's high time you learned to take no for an answer. Even in your sheltered existence you must have come across the word.' She shook her head in disgust at her loss of control and the mane of chestnut hair flew dramatically about her face. A step away, high-heeled boots clicking impatiently on the tiled floor, then she whirled round again. 'Push much further and it will come close to harassment.'

She saw she had got to him. His face had closed, lips pressed together, eyes glacial, as cold as she was roused. 'I would never have supposed that inviting a woman and her child for a few days' holiday at Disneyland could, by any stupid twisting, be interpreted as harassment. But I suppose it's all very subjective.'

'Unwelcome pursuit is harassment. Full stop.'

'Yes.' She found his weary sigh deeply affecting, especially since she was already regretting the strength of her response. 'I was simply following the male instinct. Reaching out for something I find irresistibly attractive. *You*, Ellie.' His smile was brief, grim, unamused. 'In case I'm not being particularly coherent. And I'm not about to apologise for that.' Looking away from her, he focused on the hall window with its view over the garden. 'I can't explain this feeling I have for you—even to myself I can't explain it. I just can't find the words. But I assure you, inviting you and Charlie to Paris was as much for her sake as for my own.' Another little grin. 'And I'm sorry you won't come.'

'I'm sorry too.' And she was, more sorry than she could understand. She opened her mouth to add some anodyne phrase, but before she could utter it there was an agonised wail from somewhere above their heads, a clatter of feet on polished floorboards and a small figure came hurtling down at breakneck speed, throwing herself against her mother so they both came close to collapsing.

'Darling—' Ellie was aghast. 'What on earth is the matter? Have you hurt—?'

But the face turned up towards her was transfigured, not by pain but by disappointment and misery. 'Why?' One small fist tried to stifle a sob. 'Why can't we go? Ben wants to take us to Disneyland. To Disneyland.' The voice rose several decibels at the enormity of life's disappointments. 'And you won't let us go. All the other children have been to Disneyland and I...' Words gave way to a few broken-hearted sobs while she selected the most vulnerable spot for the final thrust. 'Why don't you want me to be happy, Mummy?'

Suddenly, as if realising she had gone too far, and in front of Ben too, the loud sobbing stopped, gave way to an occasional hiccup which was stifled against her mother's shirt, while Ellie looked down stricken, heart-broken. Was this what her adored daughter really thought of her? Unconsciously her hands continued to make adjustments to the braided hair while she struggled for composure.

'Charlie.' Ben had knelt and was speaking to the child, reasonably but firmly. 'You know that's not true. I don't know you all that well, but it seems to me you have a pretty terrific mother and maybe you should say you're sorry. I know you didn't mean it—we all say things we don't mean when we're angry or disappointed. Am I right?' A slight nod and a sniffle. 'You were just upset?' Another nod and a more dramatic sob. 'And you would like to say sorry to your mother?'

'I'm sorry, Mummy.' Charlie backed away and Ellie, staring down, felt she would be the next to burst into a fit of weeping. 'I just so wanted to go on all the rides.'

'Good girl.' Ben smiled and tweaked her plait. 'And

I'm sure you'll see them all one day. Now, what about going upstairs to wash your face? Then come down as soon as possible so we can say goodbye before I go.'

'Do you have to go, Ben?' Another affecting sob.

'I really must.' He grinned again, slapped his open palm against hers. 'But, who knows? I might come back one day.'

When they were alone, Ellie found it impossible to hide her dejection and made no pretence of resistance when Ben put an arm round her and gave her a hug. 'Don't let her get you down. All of them have tantrums—it's called ''getting your own way''. I'm sorry I was the cause.'

'No.' She felt herself being drawn closer; his chin rested on top of her head. 'It was all my fault. I ought to have asked her—after all, she was invited as well.'

'No, of course you shouldn't. If you truly can't go then it would have been most unfair.' He put a finger under her chin and tilted her head. 'But are you telling me...?' His eyes searched hers with great intensity.

It was at that moment the front door swung open to show David Merriman about to drop an envelope onto the doormat. Ellie's angst was forgotten, her face now crimson with embarrassment and guilt.

David stared at the entwined figures.

'Ellie, I'm sorry I'm late with this thank-you note. Liz and I enjoyed it immensely last night. I'm sorry,' he repeated, but with a different emphasis, as he backed out and ran down the steps. They heard the car engine fire.

Last night? Those words lodged in Ellie's mind, blocking out the thought processes. What had happened last night? It seemed her whole life had been swept aside since then, her normal, relatively placid, non-threatening existence gone. Until this man had come back with an-guish in his wake to wreck everything. And for a second time.

With what firmness she could summon, she detached herself, looked up into the face which for years had tor-mented her dreams. She must find the courage to tell him to go.

CHAPTER SEVEN

'I'M SORRY, Ben.' Determined to give him no excuse for comforting her again, Ellie tried hard to be casual. It was just a pity her voice was so shaken, a dead give-away. 'I don't want to appear inhospitable, but I really do have a pile of work I must get on with...'

'And you'd like me to leave?' His smile was a mere formality. It did not reach his eyes, which were slatey grey. 'Strange how I've sensed that since our first meeting in Singapore, and all the time...I'm wondering why. I don't, as a rule, have such a scary effect on females.'

That she could easily believe, but... 'I'm sorry.' But why say the words which ought to have been in *his* mouth? He had twenty times, a hundred times more reason... 'But, as I said...'

'Yeah, you're sorry, and you're busy and you're not in the mood for any kind of relationship—though I don't know I suggested anything of the sort. Or, perhaps it's simply that you and David are involved. But sure as hell—' now he took no pains to hide his bitterness '—if I were in his position, then my idea of thanking you for dinner...or for anything else...would not be a polite little note dropped on the doormat and turning away when another man had his arms about you.'

'I shan't listen to you.' Even in her own ears she was sounding pompous. 'David Merriman has been very kind to me. It isn't every man who would be prepared to have another man's child...' she hesitated, again wondering if there was a direct accusation in her tone '…tagging along,' she finished more circumspectly.

'No—o—o.' His eyes had narrowed again. It was only too obvious that various questions were racing through his mind. 'Not every man…' Another pause, somehow more significant. 'It would depend largely on the child, even more on the mother.'

It was difficult to smile, to shrug off any implication, and she didn't think she had succeeded. 'I'm sure there's a compliment there, for Charlie as well. Thank you. And thank you for the lunch. I truly enjoyed it.'

'Mummy…' A plaintive call took their attention to the top of the stairs, then, unable to see Charlie, they located her halfway down, sitting on a step with her face pressed against the banister, looking at them.

'Charlie.' The diversion was welcome. 'How long have you been sitting there? Come down and say good-bye to Ben; I think he wants to go.' And she ignored the dry cynical sideways glance.

'Oh, Mummy.' In a moment Charlie had rushed down the last of the steps. Her arms circled her mother's waist and she gazed up with all the expressive appeal she could muster. 'If I say I'm very, very, *very* sorry, and if I promise to be as good as gold all the time, can't we go to Disneyland with Ben? Please, Mummy.'

Ellie gritted her teeth, hardened her heart and tried to conceal her irritation at such blatant manipulation. She tried to remember all her friends had told her about the sheer opportunism of children in playing one parent off against another, the fact that they could always be depended on to embarrass you in front of strangers. And she tried, for heaven's sake, not to shout and scream with frustration that she too wanted to go to Paris. More than anything else she had ever wanted in her life, if truth be told, but...

'Darling, I'll try to take you another time. Perhaps with Wendy and Linda.'

'But it would be such fun with Ben.'

'I'm not sure if the invitation is still open.' Looking at him for the first time since the interruption, Ellie silently begged for help, but his expression gave not a hint of any such intention, and by then, Charlie, sussing the situation with unnerving accuracy, had switched allegiance. She caught Ben's hand and was quite shameless in her pleading.

'Ben...' A tiny tremor, enough to convince her mother that the Royal Shakespeare Company beckoned. 'Ben, do you still want us to come to Disneyland with you?'

For a moment he looked down at her soberly before the struggle against laughter was lost. 'How I wish, Charlie Osborne, that all females were as amenable as you.' He raised an eyebrow. 'So many of them are awkward and stubborn.'

Ellie, by now feeling battered and weary in face of this war of attrition, wasn't even surprised when she heard her own voice admitting defeat. And it was only much later, when she lay sleepless in the dark of her bedroom, that she was overcome with terror at the ease with which she had surrendered to the enemy.

But by the time they reached Paris, she had made a decision. She would put all her misgivings behind her and enjoy the holiday. What point was there in doing anything else? Certainly continuing to plague herself with doubts was a futile exercise. She would act as if she had come away for a few days with friends—with

David Merriman, for example, with him and his sister, Liz. She would have been relaxed, at ease, afraid neither of David nor of her reaction to him, whereas... But it was impossible to compare the two men.

During the journey, at least, Ben Congreve had been as unthreatening as she could have wished. He even gave the impression that he had planned everything to give her daughter a treat. And, no, she felt not a hint of pique. In her mind, Ellie even likened it to a day at the seaside for underprivileged children. Though it was impossible to resist a little spleen when she saw how intimate the two were becoming. And who would have to pick up the pieces when the wonderful Ben disappeared back to the States after he discovered he could not have what he wanted? What he had paid for, in fact. Although, to be fair, she suspected even he knew that was not on the cards this time round.

The hotel where they were staying was one of Paris's most prestigious and expensive. Looking round the foyer, Ellie was for a moment intimidated by so much wealth and splendour. Even Charlie was seriously impressed, for the chatter which had been virtually non-stop since London dried up abruptly, and she clung to her mother's hand as they were escorted to the lift and whisked upstairs.

The suite she and Charlie were to share was enormous: huge twin beds, sitting room with sofas and chairs in pale leather, a large bathroom and wardrobes in which their small collection of clothes would be lost.

'I'll pick you up in about...' Ben glanced at his watch '...would half an hour be enough? We can have something to eat downstairs in the brasserie then head out to Disneyland. Or if you prefer—' over the child's head he smiled at Ellie, whose response was still slightly reluctant '—we could go straight there to eat.'

Anxiously, Charlie studied faces. 'I think going straight there, don't you, Mummy?'

'I think you might be right.' Now her smile was wholehearted, spontaneous and she bent down for a quick hug, at last admitting her own excitement. 'And are you, like me, keen to be there as soon as we can? Thank you, Ben. Half an hour would be fine.'

'Good. And you know I'm in 302—one floor up?'

Even when he had gone, his presence lingered. Ellie knew he had been stating his position, telling her she need feel no pressure, that he had not arranged adjoining rooms, there would be no demands. Just as well, since she was no longer the naive young woman who had imagined the world was her oyster. And she never would be again.

By chance—a happy chance, Ellie decided with her new-found optimism—they met Ben in the elevator on the way down. He swept her with a glance which made her heart beat a little faster, her breathing quicken, and she was glad when his attention moved at once to her daughter.

'I didn't know I was to have the pleasure of taking twins out this afternoon.'

'Silly.' The little minx fluttered her lashes, then looked down at the jade silk blouse worn on top of trousers and which matched her mother's. 'We're not really twins, Ben. But don't you think Mummy looks very pretty in that colour?'

'I could hardly have put it better myself.' Now his appraisal was unstinted, as if, having been given permission, there was no further need to hold back. 'I think it's the perfect contrast with her hair. But then…' now his expression was mischievous, conspiratorial '…I've always thought she looks pretty good whatever she wears. But guess what?' His voice dropped still lower. 'She doesn't like people saying things like that.'

Fortunately they had reached the ground floor and the embarrassing chatter came to a halt, though with so many mirrors around the place it was difficult to avoid coming to the same conclusion he had reached.

This shade, with its iridescent lights *was* good with her russetty hair, and today, matching Charlie, she had caught it back in a wide black bow. And she had been slightly more lavish than usual with make-up—this was Paris, after all. Eyeliner, discreetly applied, and intense mascara emphasised extremely striking features, and the full mouth was touched by luscious glossy plum. Already she was aware of Ben taking note.

She was looking at them walking towards this tall, slender woman, pale cotton trousers contrasting with the jade shirt, and was quite simply…looking, feeling great. And, she had to admit, with a pang, all three of them looked great: the pretty little girl, a replica of her mother, and the man, taller still, broad-shouldered, powerful, dark, confident. The kind of man used to having his own way, prepared to adopt the most underhand means of disarming resistance. His kind always did somehow… She must remember and be on guard.

But she wasn't on guard against enjoying herself, and that was what they all did in spades. Of course, a great deal of the adult pleasure derived from the child's wide-eyed enchantment, and being on guard slipped from Ellie's mind as she and Ben became conspirators in the vicarious experience, unaware that they were doing, quite simply, what came naturally to parents.

Together they ate hot dogs, licking along the edges as fried onions and tomato ketchup squeezed out of the rolls, drank root beer and sarsaparilla, and screamed in unison over some of the rides. They shook hands with more Disney characters than they could have imagined in a month of Sundays, and at the end they took the train back to the centre of the city with promises and plans for a repeat visit the following afternoon, when Ben would have finished his business affairs.

'You must be tired, Charlie.' As he spoke Ben hoisted her high in the air to perch her on his shoulders, the child not resisting but prepared to argue against the statement.

'No, Ben, I'm not. Truly I'm not.'

'Well, I guess you're the only one who isn't.' He gave a rueful sideways glance towards her mother, who shrugged in sympathetic agreement. 'And I promise you, I'm speaking for your mother as well as for myself.'

'Well, I'm not the least little bit tired,' declared Charlie, then, after a loud, prolonged yawn, giggled at herself.

As they reached the door of the suite, Ellie sighed with relief. 'What wouldn't I give for a cup of tea? All that sweet sarsaparilla is designed, I'm sure, to make you drink more of it.'

'That's the game plan.' But already he was on the telephone, dialling Room Service. Ellie heard him order tea and sandwiches, milk and biscuits, and thought how pleasant it was to have no responsibility for any arrangements.

'Oh, the bliss of sitting down and taking the weight

off.' Sinking down onto one of the blond sofas, she stretched, grinned, yawned. 'But it's been a wonderful day, Ben. Thank you for organising it so brilliantly.' A quick glance at her daughter, whose attention was now elsewhere. 'I'm sure she has never had a day like it in her life.'

He was lying back in a chair directly opposite, hands behind his head, legs stretched out, feet crossed at the ankles. 'And I could almost say the same, except...'

Except? A question lingered in her mind, but the arrival of the tea trolley was a diversion which made Ellie forget to pursue the answer.

Dinner in the very grand restaurant of the hotel was all she might have expected, quite delicious food and wine, and afterwards they walked along the Champs-Elysées until it became clear that Charlie was having difficulty trailing one foot past the other and a cab was summoned to take them back.

Ben, who had been waiting in the sitting room while Ellie put her daughter to bed, stood when she came in. 'I was hoping that maybe you'd like to go down to the bar for a drink. There is—'

'Oh, no.' Her refusal was automatic and nervy, even in Charlie's presence, strolling along the boulevards, she had been conscious of all kinds of sensations which must be kept under control, and now they were alone the situation was still more fraught. 'No, I couldn't possibly leave her alone in a strange place.'

He took his seat opposite, his eyes dark and full of seductive reflections—dangerously seductive reflections from the lamps positioned about the room. 'I was about to say there is a child-sitting service and—'

'No, really, I'd rather not.'

'And we needn't be long.'

'In any case—' she tried to smile, difficult when she was having this very disturbing reaction, where every nerve in her body might have been honed and polished '—like Charlie, I'm rather tired. But why...?'

'Yes, I guess you're right.' His smile was taut. 'And I'm picking up those vibes again.'

He was about to get up when she stopped him—purely a reaction against her guilt complex. After all, they had had a wonderful day. It was so obvious that he liked Charlie and she certainly liked him, which could mean problems in the not too distant future, but...

'I was going to say...' Even as she spoke she knew it was a mistake; giving the green light was against her plan. 'If you want a drink, why not have something from the fridge? It's crammed with all kinds of things.'

'Well...' Even he was doubtful, and stood for a second looking down at her. 'If you will have one too.'

'I'd love something cold and fizzy and thirst-quenching.'

'Right.' Still he gave the impression of reluctance to move while she was suddenly enjoying herself, enjoying the relaxed way she was lying back on the sofa, surrounded with piles of soft cushions. Her full dark skirt was spread out and the filmy white blouse gave tantalising glimpses of skin, the two-strand pearl choker drawing attention to her throat. She was being quite uncharacteristically skittish, and on impulse slid her feet out of the patent pumps, stretching full length on the sofa like some seductive star in an old-time movie but with only half a notion of how seductive she was being. 'A nice cold drink, please, Ben.'

His expression was inscrutable, but he said nothing as

he went into the hallway, returning a moment later with a small tray, two glasses and a gold-topped bottle from which he proceeded to peel back the foil.

'Ben! No!' Now she jerked herself upright, one foot searching for a shoe as a modicum of sense returned. 'I didn't mean you to open a bottle of champagne. We can't possibly drink all that.'

'I'm not suggesting we do.' He had filled the glasses, one of which was being held out to her, and she had no choice but to accept. 'But I think it's an occasion for champagne after all, don't you?'

'I...I can't imagine why you should say that.'

'To you, Ellie.' He sipped, his eyes sending messages she did not want to receive. 'And to one of the best days I've had for a long...for a *very* long time.'

'Thank you again for arranging it. I'm sure it's the best day Charlie has had in the whole of her life.'

'And to all your secrets, Ellie.' Now he was smiling, so she had no idea whether there was any underlying meaning in the words. 'Which I mean to decipher in the end.'

'And how boring that would be for you.' She sipped, huge eyes surveying him over the rim of her glass. This was a game she'd better learn to play.

He took the seat opposite. She had the impression he was being very careful to keep his distance, to give no reason for complaint. A good thing too. With great care she put her glass on the table. A good thing, and yet...a little frustrating. She might have enjoyed continuing the game a little longer, reminding him that she had the upper hand.

'And you, Ellie?' His words interrupted her contradictory musings.

'What?' The silvery eyes widened dramatically as she tried to fix her mind on an answer. 'I'm sorry…'

'No, I'm sorry.' He grinned. 'I was trying to pin you down, trying to make you admit you too had had one of your best days ever, but I shan't insist. It was enough—' He broke off, stared with a change of mood down into his glass before draining it.

'Enough…?' She prompted.

'It was enough to see you laugh, to see you give every indication that you were having a good time…'

'I was.' A show of indignation backed up by a reproving laugh. 'Of course I was. I *can* enjoy myself, you know, even though you have this mistaken idea that I can't.'

'I know you can. If I had any doubts then today has killed them off.' He rose, picked up the bottle, and a moment later both glasses had been refilled. 'I'm glad,' he said simply as he took his seat again. 'But, tell me, Ellie, how long have you and Charlie been on your own?'

'My husband…' It was all so remote it had taken on an air of unreality. 'My husband Greg died soon after Charlie was born.' Best to stick to the truth as far as possible, reduce the chances of mistakes later on. Not that there was going to be a 'later on' as far as Ben was concerned.

'That must have been pretty tough on you.'

But how much tougher without Greg willing to protect her. Now, at this distance, it was hard to understand why it had seemed important to shield her parents from the shame. And how pointless, since it was the kind of thing impossible to conceal, even at a distance, and she had found it a great relief to tell her father most of the truth

when he had flown to London. Her mother had been told
an edited version, and they had both forgiven her and
had understood her actions.

'It was tough.' At last she remembered he was waiting
for an answer. 'But if he had lived, Greg would have
been an invalid, which he would have hated.' Her eyes
grew shadowy, wistful.

'And Charlie? Has she never missed having a father?'

'Well, we speak of him, but since she has never
known what it is to have a father, perhaps she misses
him less than we imagine. But, oh—' it was a cry from
the heart which would have been easy for him to mis-
construe '—how I miss him for her.'

'You must miss him very much.' When there was no
answer to that he went on with just a shade of hesitation,
'And have you never wanted to remarry, Ellie? I'd have
thought being happily married once might encourage
you to try again.'

How dared he make assumptions? What right...?
'Does that mean that you, having been less than happily
married, would never take another risk?'

The sharpness of her manner brought a change, shut-
ters came down, but when he spoke his voice was still
controlled, unemotional. 'It would have to be an irresistible urge, but I guess the answer to your question is
no. I keep hoping. What was it some guy said about
second marriages? ''The triumph of hope over experience''?' He grinned, his face lighting up. 'That is certainly not my opinion.'

Ellie raised her glass to her mouth, and, unexpectedly
amused by the reference, smiled at him from beneath
her long lashes.

'And…David Merriman has never tempted you to try again?'

David! Mention of his name wiped out any inclination to smile, and the glass hit the table with a thump. 'Damn you, why do you insist in bringing his name up?' And making me feel guilty about being here with you, neglecting my business, annoying my friends.

When she had rung to tell him of the proposed trip to Paris, David had been less than enthusiastic. 'I wouldn't have thought that was your sort of thing, Ellie. If I had known, I would have been happy to take you,' had been more or less his exact, rather stiff words.

She returned to Ben Congreve. 'David and Liz have been friends since they came to the village three years ago. I have no idea whether or not he wishes to remarry; it's not a matter I would raise since I consider it none of my business. I do know he was happily married and was devastated when his wife died about five years ago, so perhaps he has no inclination. Lots of people can live without sex, you know.'

Her eyes flashed angrily and the mane of hair, backlit, seemed to glow with energy, but the instant she heard her words she longed to recall them. There was a silence while she waited for his next move.

'And you, Ellie?' He raised his glass, seemed fascinated by the contents before he replaced it, looking directly across. 'Do you find it easy to live without sex?'

Since her last unguarded remark she had been waiting, heart in a state of agitation, for his comeback, and now she felt the colour hit her cheeks. Her eyes blazed as she remembered what she had been condemned to. And by this man, who had the gall to put the question. Not only had Charlie been denied her father, but *she* had been

deprived of the love for which she yearned. For which
she had never stopped yearning. And Ben Congreve had
put the question. How dared he?

At last she found a note of icy disdain. 'That I do live
without it is an assumption on your part. As far as I
know, marriage is not a prerequisite.' And it pleased her
to see his stony expression was immediately preceded
by a flash of something like sheer fury, and it was a
moment before he spoke, this time to her averted profile.
But her pleasure was short-lived. She looked up in alarm
as she felt him slip into the seat alongside; he actually
smiled, as if her reaction was the one he had hoped for.

'You are quite right.' Although he didn't touch her
she was extremely aware of and made nervous by the
arm extended along the back of the settee. If she were
to lean back...which of course she had no intention of
doing... 'I was being presumptuous. But I asked merely
because I was interested...and you have been so very
careful to give the impression that you find my company
distasteful. No?' He responded to her slight contradictory sound. 'Well, should I say, uncomfortable, perhaps?' Now the gleaming eyes were amused, intrigued,
taking note of the passionate rise and fall of her breast
due, if only he knew, more to his closeness than any
actual words...

'There are so many things about you, Ellie, which are
both irritatingly elusive and reassuringly familiar. I want
to find out all about you, to discover a clue to this intense
relationship, for I'm pretty sure...'

His gaze was now so dominating she had no power
to look elsewhere, no power to move aside as his hand
came up to brush a strand of hair from her forehead, no
power to hide the shiver as his fingers lingered against

her cheek. For a moment it seemed her heart would burst with agitation. And with pleasure. Oh, yes, impossible to deny the intensity of that pleasure, and in listening to the voice too, with all its mellow cadences.

'I'm pretty sure you feel it as much as I do. This…this nebulous but very powerful empathy…'

This was something she had to interrupt. There was danger in allowing him to continue. She owed it to herself, to Charlie… She smiled with just the right touch of condescension. 'I think this is the writer speaking. You're determined to make life imitate art, or vice versa, and life isn't like that at all.'

'This—' his hand moved, touched her upper arm, fingers caressing lightly, scorching through the delicate lawn '—is nothing to do with fiction. This is your life. Mine. But what I can't work out, Ellie, is why, when you have so many adverse feelings, you are here in the first place.'

That brought her out of any daydream she might—*might*—have been devising. She sat up, dislodging his hand. Away with that tormenting, teasing touch or she would never be able to stand up to him. 'Why am I here?' Even to her own ears she sounded shrill, maybe even shrewish. She took a moment to regain control and then spoke with determined moderation. 'How can you ask? I'm here because you deliberately tempted my daughter. That is why I'm here and for no other reason.' Her glare did not intimidate, and he took his time replying to her accusation.

'It won't wash, Ellie.' Her indrawn breath made him smile ruefully. 'It simply won't wash. Firstly, Charlie overhearing was an accident—a lucky one for me, I agree, but you know it wasn't planned. And besides, if you didn't want to come, truly did not want to be in my company, why are we here?'

'Because…' she began in a rush of hot indignation, anger that he refused to understand her position. 'Because I couldn't bear to disappoint her. It would not have been fair.'

'You could have made up for that easily by bringing her by yourself, or even one of your friends might have been happy to come with you.'

'If, by "one of your friends" you mean David, why not say so?'

It was difficult to decide from his manner whether he was amused or deadly serious. 'I suppose the name sticks in my throat because I'm insanely jealous of the man.'

'Wh-what?' Hard to believe, but she thought he had said… 'What did you say?'

'You heard.' He spoke harshly. 'It's a feeling I've not experienced before, and I'm finding it hard to deal with. But I'm waiting for a credible explanation. Why are you here with me, now?'

Impossible to give an answer since there was none. If she were to tell the truth she would be humiliated, and if she lied… So, it was best to shrug, to look bewildered.

'Isn't it strange?' He spoke confidentially, as if the situation were genuinely intriguing. 'You don't know why you're here, whereas I'm perfectly clear on the matter. I'm here with you and Charlie because this is the one place in the world I want to be. And although Charlie is adorable, it's really all to do with you. I'm here, Ellie, because, quite simply, I want you.' And somehow, when he reached out for her, she leaned back against the cushions as if she had been waiting for him.

There was an aching yearning inside as his lips brushed hers, once, twice, transporting her back to that beach in the Windwards. Soft air was stirring the tiny hairs on her arms to an electrifying awareness. She was pulling that dark, bearded face towards her, rejoicing in the power she had over him, still more in his over her. Her eyes were drifting closed, fingers twisting in the dark hair and…

It didn't last. Well, nothing lasts, does it? she acknowledged blankly as he drew away from her, looking down, mocking himself—or her. Hard to tell. But he was seriously disturbed, that much was clear in the way he was struggling for control. At last he spoke.

'Now, don't tell me, Ellie—don't tell me you didn't want to come to Paris with me. That kiss, like the one the other day, tells a whole different story. You want to be here with me just as much as I want to be with you. And your daughter is merely an excuse. For both of us. So sleep on it. I promise you, I shall want answers to these points before too long.'

Almost before she was aware of it, he had gone, and the door closed with a soft click. She was left there with her frustration, her heart beating wildly against her ribcage. He wanted her. That was what he'd said. He wanted her, so…so why for heaven's sake hadn't he taken her when she had made it so clear…?

When at last she had been prepared to admit she was as obsessed with Ben Congreve as she had ever been. And for that she despised herself.

CHAPTER EIGHT

By ALL the rules, next morning's encounter ought to have meant agonising embarrassment over the *café au lait*, and it was doubly irritating that his greeting was so matter-of-fact—not even a query as to how she had slept. Badly, as it happened.

Ellie added a dab of black cherry conserve to her croissant and popped it into her mouth. How really satisfying it would have been to flail him with the truth, to tell him that his actions last night, her persuasive invitations to lovemaking had, when he'd failed to follow through, had the most devastating, frustrating effect on her sleep pattern... She glared across, further incensed to find the other two deep in plans for the day. And without much reference to her. Of course.

'So,' he was saying, 'since I'm going to be tied up for most of the morning, you might want to go out to the park. I could meet you for a late lunch and...'

'Yes, please,' Charlie was breathless. 'Lunch where they do those all-day cowboy meals.'

'Well, if that suits everyone.' This time a less perfunctory look towards Ellie. 'But maybe... Would you prefer a morning's shopping, Ellie? You've seen little of Paris, and if you insist on going home tomorrow...?'

'Yes.' Ellie, suddenly struck by the enormity of her decision to abandon her business for the sake of a few days' pleasure, replied automatically. 'Yes, I have so much work piling up.'

How, then, to explain this deep-seated reluctance to face her real world again? She ought never to have come in the first place, but it was impossible to whip up feelings of genuine regret. Just one look at her daughter's face was enough to confirm that she had been right to come. Her own reactions did not come into it.

Charlie could not hide her anxiety. 'Oh, I don't think you will want to look at boring old dress shops, will you, Mummy?'

'You think not?' Ben regarded her seriously. 'You think she'd rather spend the whole day at Disneyland?'

'Yes.' Breathless uncertainty, which assured Ellie there was no way she could deprive Charlie of the full measure of enjoyment. And with a sudden mood swing her eyes caught Ben's in unguarded delight.

'You see, there is simply no contest.' Even as she spoke the words she was regretting the casual impulse which had encouraged his eyes to grow more intimate, reminding her, reminding him, of the previous night, lips curving in appreciation which had nothing to do with the pleasure they were giving Charlie.

Ellie found the morning slightly more tedious than the previous day, and sat down with relief in the saloon where they had arranged to meet Ben at lunchtime. 'There he is.' Charlie was the first to spot him shouldering his way through the swing doors, and she jumped up, ran to him, was lifted high in the air before being set back on her feet. For a moment they stood, his head bent, chatting, laughing, flirting, before they turned and he allowed himself to be pulled towards her table. His eyes sought her out, adding to the ache in her chest...

'Mummy...' Charlie was still laughing, excited. 'Ben

almost made a mistake. He thought at first I was Jess and…'

Jess? The name of his niece? Ellie froze. Her eyes glazed over so she no longer saw the linen jacket she liked so much, the darker polo neck. He had become a stranger, a threat…

'That's not very likely.' Her voice, when at last she found it, was brittle, defensive and even a little shrill. 'That's not very likely, is it?' To prevent a shiver she pressed her teeth together.

'Ellie?' His voice was puzzled, questioning, and even without looking she knew he was frowning, but Charlie was hurrying on with her story.

'Ben said Jess wears exactly the same clothes as I do.' Complacently she looked down at her denims and checked shirt. 'He says it's what most people wear in Montana.'

'Oh?' There was little she could add. She could not explain her sudden panic, except that she had thought as they came closer how right they looked together, though the implication of that thought was something she did not wish to explore. And he was bound to wonder…

Pondering the delights of Red Flannel Hash against Louisiana Squab 'n' Beans, Ben found it difficult to keep his thoughts on the menu. It was impossible for him to dismiss from his mind the image of Ellie's stricken face, one moment so tender and relaxed, the next as if her very life was about to be forfeit. He was trying to re-member what might have caused it…but at least she seemed to have recovered enough to give her order.

When the waitress had gone, he put out a hand and touched hers. 'Had a hard time?' he asked quietly.

'No, of course not.' For a moment, certain that her

fears would be written clearly on her features, she avoided him. 'We've had a great time, haven't we, Charlie?' Then, feeling her courage return, she smiled at him. 'Why do you ask?'

'Oh…' He frowned. 'Just a feeling—as if ghosts had come back to haunt you. But now I'm starving. What about you, Charlie?'

The rest of the day passed more or less as the first. Charlie was captivated by the magical world they had entered, and the adults, they too were in a state of mild enchantment which Ellie put down to the vicarious pleasure of watching Charlie. Those unnerving few minutes back in the café she dismissed as an aberration, which she hoped Ben had forgotten by now, though when she turned to him with a smiling expression she found him looking at her assessingly, as if still pondering her strange behaviour.

And then it seemed he keyed in to her altered mood. His mouth curved upwards, his eyes lightened, held hers.

'Ellie.' He spoke her name as if to himself, as if savouring the sound, and coincidentally caused a potent throb deep in the pit of her stomach. 'Ellie…' It was repeated with such yearning that she felt the breath being sucked from her body. She could look nowhere but into his eyes. 'You've no idea how long I've been searching for you.'

The words brought her back to earth with a bump. Her eyes grew wary and she turned away, making a play of looking for Charlie. 'I've no idea what you mean, Ben. Where were you searching for us? You knew where we were; we met up at the arranged spot.' Then she turned back with a carefully raised eyebrow and an amused, perplexed expression.

'That's not what I mean and you know it. And it was you I was looking for. Singular.'

'Oh, I see.' Not his own daughter, then—so, what was new? All along she had known that was not on his agenda. *Have your fling and dismiss it from your mind* seemed to be his—most men's—motto. Searchingly she stared, determined to find in his features some reflection of the basic character flaw. With no success. 'I still don't understand what you mean.'

If her voice had grown sharper he appeared not to notice. His answer was slow. And rather thoughtful.

'Neither do I, Ellie. And to tell the truth, I find that more than a little disturbing.'

Fortunately they were rescued by Charlie, who came back at that moment, breathlessly demanding that they move on to the Mickey Mouse theme shop, where she could buy some presents to take home. She seemed not to notice that the adults were quieter than usual.

But by the time they sat down to dinner that night Ellie, at least, had thrust aside all adverse feelings. There was no reason to deny Ben the credit for bringing them here. It had turned out to be the most wonderful holiday for Charlie, one she would remember for the rest of her life. As to the cost…Ellie repressed a shudder. Luxury-class hotel, all these outings. In spite of what she had heard of the fabulous sums earned by top writers… He just had no idea how ordinary people lived.

'I'm sorry we have to go back to England tomorrow, aren't you, Charlie?' Waiting for her answer, Ellie could imagine he was enjoying teasing both of them.

'Yes, I'm *so* sorry. But—' intercepting a warning glance, she altered her tone '—I've had the bestest time ever Ben. Thank you for bringing us. All my friends will be so jealous.' The thought was clearly something to be savoured.

'Oh?' Ben frowned. 'That's strange.' And, when Charlie looked up enquiringly, 'I thought you said all your friends had been to Disneyland.'

'I didn't.'

'You did.' Two voices spoke at once, with Ellie going on to underline the point. 'Quite distinctly you said everyone had been there except you.'

'Oh, that…' Charlie tried to look casual but was let down by a blush. 'Well, not exactly everyone.' And she joined in the laughter.

'I tell you what, Charlie, did you know there's a swimming pool downstairs in the basement?'

'I didn't know that.'

'Well, since we're leaving tomorrow right after breakfast, why don't we meet before breakfast and have a swim before we set off? A pity never to use the pool. We could have a last fling before the end of the holiday.'

'Yes.' Her eyes were gleaming. 'Can I, Mum?'

'You may,' her mother corrected. 'The only problem is, you haven't brought a swimsuit.'

'That's OK. There's a shop where we can buy one,' said Ben.

'And Mummy can come too?'

'Of course.' His eyes were impassive. 'You do swim, I imagine?'

This, from the man who had once compared her to a mermaid, struck her silent for a second or two.

'Ellie?'

'Yes, I swim. Or at least I used to. But…' Impossible to explain her reluctance to appear before him in a bikini—even supposing she had one with her. 'But I think on this occasion I shall pass. You two can swim while I do the packing.' She paused, something in her manner holding his attention, until she continued. 'Do you still sail, Ben?'

She had no idea what had made her pose the question. Was it some kind of bravado which insisted she drop an oblique hint? Or had the words slipped out, unconsidered until it was too late? The instant they were spoken she wanted to recall them, especially when she saw his expression change, become more watchful.

'Sail?' At last he spoke. 'I don't ever recall mentioning the subject to you.'

'Oh, didn't you?' She averted her head to disguise the panic. 'Then maybe someone else. Jenny or Robert, I imagine.'

'No.' He was frowning. 'I don't think so.'

'Or perhaps I read an article?' She was floundering.

'Mmm.' He was unimpressed. 'But, since you take pride in never having heard of Jonas Parnell, I think it's unlikely, don't you?' And before she could think of anything to say he answered her first question. 'But the answer is, no, I no longer sail.'

There was a longish pause before he returned to the original subject, telling Charlie he would pick her up before eight the following morning, and then he continued, 'But now you look as if you're going to fall asleep over that chocolate mousse, and I was wondering... How would it be if your mother and I went for a walk round Paris? We could arrange for someone to stay in the sitting room.'

'Well...' The child was thoughtful. 'If she's a nice babysitter—as nice as Wendy.'

'Darling, we're not going to find someone as nice as

Wendy, but I'm sure she'll be nice. Different, of course, but you can compare them tomorrow on the way home—tell us all about her.'

Ellie knew she ought to have been discouraging—after all, she too was tired, much too tired to go wandering about Paris with Ben, and besides, there was the implication that he would want the answers to some of the questions he had posed the previous night. And, more pertinent of all, he might return to the subject of sailing. Clearly it was something which had disturbed him. If he did, then her only way out would be to plead amnesia, insist that after all it must have come from Jenny.

Easy to feel confident about that sitting in the busy restaurant. Less so when, Charlie comfortably settled with the babysitter—a Canadian girl who was working her way round Europe—she and Ben left the security of the large hotel and began to stroll along the boulevards.

It was a perfect evening: dark sky strewn with stars, a slip of moon peeping behind the trees, the air fresh and clean with just a hint of autumn crispness. Dry leaves rustled in a faint breeze, reflected lights gleamed on the water as boats plied back and forth.

For dinner, Ellie had worn a full, midi-length skirt, silky and swaying, and for the walk had topped it with a short lemon-coloured jacket, a stand-up collar framing her glowing face.

His arm came round her as they leaned against a low pale stone wall, watching the river traffic, and though she shivered it was more excitement than apprehension, and she did not draw back, allowing his hand to rest on her hip when they moved on.

It was hard to admit that all the old feelings were being rekindled in this different time, different place.

And there was something about the magic of this city, where every few yards lovers were exchanging kisses, talking softly beneath the sheer, soaring beauty of the floodlit Notre Dame, a city of sheer magic, where even the names—the Seine, the Louvre, the Madeleine—the words on the tongue heightened emotions to a dangerous level.

Immersed in these thoughts, Ellie looked up in alarm when, reaching a quiet spot, Ben swung her round to face him.

'It's all right.' His manner, though tolerant, held an undertow of danger which she would ignore at her peril, but she felt a stab of sympathy—for both of them perhaps. 'You needn't look so apprehensive.'

'I don't think I was.'

'Unsure of yourself, then.' And yet to him it seemed this woman had never been unsure of herself. Reserved, of course—to the point of being withdrawn. Though he would swear there was nothing cold about her. Suspicious, certainly, and he would dearly love to know what had brought that about. There seemed little in her background... Or was it only with him? He had seen her at ease with others and it was painful to imagine, but why, in God's name? Why, when his own reaction was so entirely opposite? Why, when he found her so disturbingly beautiful?

Obeying an intense yearning, he brushed a thumb over the full soft lips, saw them tremble, watched the liquid expression in her eyes darken with what in someone else might have been passion. 'Or scared perhaps?'

'Nor scared.'

'I must tell you, Ellie...I hope you know already…you have no reason in the world to be scared of me.'

Looking at him, she wished with all her heart and soul that was the truth. Oh, not in the simple sense, not if she were to behave rationally, but if ever she were to forget, to respond as every fibre of her body was urging her to do now, then he posed the greatest danger in the world, and so her manner was carefully, even insultingly bland. 'I told you, Ben, I'm not scared. I don't see you as a threat.'

And deliberately she moved away, breaking the contact, one part of her mind almost amused by her ability to remain detached, giving no sign of the inner ferment. But the other, the emotional side, was distracted by the need to escape from the torment and yearnings for what might have been.

But she had brought it all on herself. This time she had no one else to blame. This time she had walked in with both eyes wide open. In her foolish simplicity she had imagined she would remain in control, but now, in this setting, almost as beguiling as the Caribbean, her own weakness was exposed.

Perhaps even more than in the Caribbean, for the controlled, sophisticated person she had become was finding it increasingly difficult to maintain the neutral position she had promised herself. *That* thought was nerve-racking enough to make her whirl round, to demand they return at once to the hotel.

'Ellie?' His eyes narrowed and he frowned.

'I must get back to Charlie; she needs me.' Another lie. The Canadian girl had inspired total confidence.

A moment later he had called a cab and they drove back to the Place de la Concorde in total silence.

When they reached the suite, they found the babysitter curled up on the sofa with a paperback book, the television on and Charlie sound asleep in bed. Nervously, agitated in a way she could not explain, Ellie went into the bedroom, touched the child's cool forehead, returned to the sitting room and slumped onto a chair, vaguely hearing Ben thanking the girl and saying goodnight.

Then he returned, took the seat opposite, watching, willing her to look at him, which at last she found impossible to avoid.

'I'm sorry.' A touch of aggression in her voice, then back to the television, focusing on the now silent head on the screen, eyes blurry, unseeing. Fiercely she bit at her lower lip. 'Put it down to the one-parent-family syndrome. We always, but *always*,' she flashed, as if he had contradicted her, 'feel worried and guilty.'

'But not when you're in the Far East.' His coolness came close to accusation, shocking her, since before he had been so endlessly sympathetic.

'What?' Her brain seized temporarily, and she frowned with the effort of concentration.

'I said…' Languidly he reached over, picked up the remote control and switched off the picture. 'Not when you're jetting round the world on your business jaunts.'

She understood then. She refused to take criticism from a permanently absent father, but fortunately she drew breath before she could blurt out that accusation. 'Without my "business jaunts", as you describe them—' her tone was lacerating '—I don't see how we could exist. Unless you think we should turn to the state for support. Would that be your idea of a solution?'

'No. No, I think people are generally much happier if they support themselves.'

It hurt Ellie that he was looking at her with something approaching dislike. He had no right, she was the one who had had to pay...

'You were the one who brought the matter up. My only comment is that you can go away for days at a time and yet this evening—after a long and, I think, happy day for Charlie, when we have made all the arrangements for her safety—you can't allow yourself an hour in the evening to walk along the banks of the Seine. To relax, for heaven's sake, to be yourself for once, not simply Charlie's mother. That, I think, is carrying martyrdom too far.'

The words stung. She struggled with the overwhelming desire to throw them back at him, to wipe the criticism from his face by explaining a few home truths. But in the end she chose to be more subtle, selecting her words in a way calculated to hurt—not that she could ever wound as he had wounded her, but she would have a damned good try.

'It's not martyrdom, caring for your own child, Ben.' A tiny smile, a patronising shake of her head. 'That's where so many people who choose not to have children get it wrong; they simply cannot understand. To have a child with someone you love to the point of madness...' Another wondering move of her head had the hair billowing about her face, and an uncontrived dreamy expression illuminated her features as she warmed to her theme. 'That changes life completely so you are never quite the same again. The old, self-indulgent, carefree, freewheeling days have gone for ever.' The schmaltzy tone rang a warning note. No need to go overboard completely. 'As I said, unless you've been there, done it, you just cannot know...'

From him there was no immediate answer. He sat, apparently relaxed, skilfully hiding the stabbing pain her words caused, trying to block from his mind the image she had aroused, unwilling to admit even to himself such tearing jealousy. But he remained intent and watchful, his eyes never leaving her face.

The silence continued for so long Ellie found herself becoming agitated again. Her heart was echoing in her ears and she was conscious of the tension, unambiguously and powerfully sexual, stretching between them. The tip of her tongue slid over parted lips. She was aware that every breath she drew was being recorded, analysed. It was a great relief—she thought it *must* be relief—when he moved, indicated he was about to leave.

'I'm sure what you say is right. No one who hasn't had children can fully understand the intensity of the relationship. But at the same time that very intensity can be a danger. I would have thought it best to relax a little, not to be too anxious all the time. This evening, after all, we did everything even the most careful parents can do...'

'Wh—?' His use of the plural brought her head up with a jerk. 'What on earth do you mean?'

He sighed, doubtless finding her query tedious. 'I mean,' he said, with a wry expression, 'you did everything the most caring parent could do. And you gave the impression of being happy with the arrangements, until suddenly you throw a top-of-the-range panic and we come rushing back for no reason. All I'm suggesting is, there's a danger that some of your anxiety will rub off on Charlie, that she'll grow up over-protected and—'

Any criticism of her role as mother rankled, and she wanted him to understand that. 'A moment ago you were saying the reverse, that I go jetting off with never a care for her. You can't have it both ways.' Her glower was rewarded by a slight smile, that familiar little shrug which conceded a point.

'Well, you know why I said that.' Disappointment now, as she saw him rise to his feet. 'I was angry with you.' He held out an apologetic hand and she, quite without thinking, put hers into it, was pulled with relentless determination to her feet. 'Incandescent.' His voice was low, throbbingly intimate. 'Furious that, rather than walk with me along some of the most magical romantic boulevards in the world, you couldn't wait to rush back to the hotel.'

She must hang onto her senses, but it was heartbreakingly difficult with him so close, her nostrils filled with the scent of him, those dark eyes so determined to dominate. 'It was simply that I had to check…'

But before she could finish whatever excuse she had meant to concoct, his mouth closed on hers and every sensible thought, every sensible, protective idea, was driven from her mind. Did he but know, she was as vulnerable to his attraction as she had been all those years ago on the Windwards.

And, for a moment, so co-operative was she that they might have been whisked back to that magical era. There was wonder at such intense pleasure, at the sheer bliss, the self-indulgence of being moulded into the curve of a powerful male body, and she allowed her hands to reach about his neck, to tangle in his hair.

For heaven's sake, she allowed her lips to part for his, felt her insides melt at the exquisite exploring contact. And then there was no question of her allowing anything; it was outside her control. All the raging needs which had for so many years been carefully damped down were flaring towards a wild explosion. His arm was tightening with the urgency and the need for possession, her feet practically leaving the floor.

'Ellie…' Their mouths parted. Ben trailed a stream of urgent kisses the length of her cheek, reached her neck. She held her head back to indicate surrender. 'Ellie, God…such longings. Since the first day we met I've dreamed…'

But at that moment she had little interest in words. All she wanted was to feel these mind-blowing sensations… Every caution, every warning was abandoned instantly as she searched again for his mouth, surrendering hers to this impatient lover. His hand slipped lower, urging her into closer contact. And soon all sense, all the hard lessons from the past, began to slide from her brain. Her breath quickened. She heard herself murmur his name in a tone of such urgent pleading and impatience it could only be giving him one unmistakable message…

'Mummy.'

The distant cry was barely heard, so totally was she in thrall to this man, to this moment, to the uncontrollable urge of her body and… And then again, as she was about to sink onto the sofa, taking him with her, that same sound—*distrait*, unwelcome, close… And the bedroom door was opening and a small figure stood there. She was yawning and trailing by one hand the teddy bear Ben had bought for her that day out at the park.

'Mummy.' Another cracking yawn, and Charlie blinked as she took in the unusual scene, accepting it with apparent composure. 'I had a bad dream.' A tiny sob.

'Oh, darling.' It was the intervention Ellie might have prayed for. Releasing herself instantly, she spared one

searing look at the man, who relinquished her with reluctance. The same man who had seduced her when she
was a mere girl and who had changed little. How dared
he? How dared he come between mother and child? How
dared he distract and bewitch her. Nothing else could
explain...

'Darling...' Her heart was still thudding uncomfort-
ably, her senses were all to pot and she felt like scream-
ing with frustration. So she made a great play of brushing the disordered hair back from the child's forehead,
speaking to the man without quite looking at him. 'I
think you'd better go, Ben. It may take some time to get
Charlie off to sleep again.'

'A very touching scene.' And when she turned to glare
he looked so cynical, so amused, she knew she had been
over-acting, even admitted to a glimmer of respect that
he had seen through her tactics. A blush started, spread
to the roots of her titian hair. She averted her profile as
he went on. 'But putting children to sleep is something
I'm expert on—lots of practice even though I'm not a
parent.'

Then, seeming to take pity on Ellie's embarrassment,
he hunkered down beside their daughter, his voice softer,
noticeably more indulgent. 'Come on now, Charlie, let
me carry you back to bed and tuck you in. It would be
awful if you were too tired in the morning to make our
date at the swimming pool. I want to see that running
dive you were telling me about.'

Running dive! Ellie followed them into the bedroom,
vaguely heard him say something about the family on
the Montana ranch. Running *flop* would be a better description of the so-called dive. She listened with the
usual mix of pain and pleasure as he went on.

'...a whole lot bigger than most of the farms in

England. In the winter they have lots of snow and go skiing. Have you ever skied, Charlie?'

'No. Once Mummy took me sledging, though.'

'Well, I think you would find it fun learning. Maybe one day you'll come for a visit. You and Jess can…'

Impossible to allow this to continue. She was incensed. In a minute he and Charlie would between them have arranged dates and flights, and when she, the restraining influence, was obliged to nip all this nonsense in the bud, it would be the devil's own job bringing Charlie back down to earth. *She* would be the stony-hearted spoiler, left to pick up the pieces. As usual. 'Time to go to sleep, Charlie, say goodnight to Ben now…'

'Goodnight, Ben.' Already her eyes were closing. 'And don't forget the morning. I can swim even if I don't know if I can ski…'

'I shan't forget.' Charlie turned to burrow deeper into the pillows and Ben brushed a hand over the tumble of hair. 'Goodnight, honey. Sleep tight.' His voice was warm, so reassuring for a child. The mother felt vulnerable. A warning, she told herself impatiently, that she ought to get this man out of her suite right now. And out of her life. Turning, she led the way from the bedroom and, rather pointedly, into the hall.

His raised eyebrow told her that the gambit had registered. 'I shall call for Charlie at about eight. You won't change your mind and come with us?'

'No—no, thank you.' Uneasily, she averted her eyes, concentrating her attention on something beyond his left shoulder. 'I shall get on with some packing. But if I do finish in time, I shall take the lift down to see how you are getting on.'

'Fine.' His hand reached for the doorknob. 'Then

sleep well, Ellie.' The door opened a fraction. 'But don't think you're going to get rid of me so easily. You and I have something to finish.' Alarmed, she flicked her eyes back to that dominating expression. 'Something we started…' his pause might have been designed to tease and torment '…in there.' A nod of his head. 'Before your daughter so inopportunely disturbed us. And don't ever again try to persuade me that you are immune from all the emotions which govern the rest of mankind. That little interlude proved the reverse, without the shadow of a doubt.'

He bent his head then, and she was afraid he was about to kiss her, began to prepare herself for another onslaught, but he merely brushed his mouth against hers—his mouth which could promise such delight. And deliver. 'I've played patient long enough. And now—' his voice roughened '—I plan to show how badly you have miscalculated. And before either of us is very much older.'

He was gone before she realised he had opened the door, and she was left with the threat hanging in the air. Leaning against it, Ellie realised her legs were trembling. One hand went up to touch her lips, which still felt sensitive and swollen. She had the defeatist thought that if he should decide to make a determined assault, far from repelling it, she would aid and abet him. Her own reaction to the forays he had already made told her as much.

In short, all her confidence had gone, and she had the dire feeling at the pit of her stomach that she would put up as much resistance as last time round. Or even less.

CHAPTER NINE

POTTERING about the bedroom next morning, after Ben had collected Charlie, Ellie tried not to admit to herself that she was depressed. All through the night she had tossed and turned, tormented by the decision she had to make.

Having reached it, she ought to have felt pleased that the equivocation was behind her. After they returned to Little Transome, life would go back to the slightly humdrum routine which had served them so well in recent years. And this interlude would simply recede to the back of her mind, as all memories did in the end. That decision ought to have been a source of relief rather than the sense of doom which she was experiencing right now.

'Mummy.' Hearing them at the door was a distraction from the bleakness of her thoughts. She folded up her nightie, placing it on top of her case before going into the hall to welcome them back. 'Mummy!' Charlie could not hide her enthusiasm. 'I wish you could have come. You would have seen my very best dive. Ben showed me how to curl my toes over the edge and fall forward, and you know what?' She giggled and flashed a flirtatious glance upwards. 'I almost—*almost*,' she emphasised, eyes sparkling, 'lost the bottom of my bikini.'

'Oh.' Ellie glanced in amusement at the tall figure standing just inside the doorway, his face half hidden in the shadows. 'How embarrassing. I did think that one was slightly on the large side.'

'But I didn't like the others. Now I have to dry my hair.' And she rushed in the direction of the bathroom.

'Wait until I come, Charlie.' Ellie turned to Ben, suddenly noticing how quiet and withdrawn he seemed. 'She appears to be full of it.' Her smile faded. 'She has been all right?'

'Yes, she's been fine.'

But he was frowning—impossible to decide what was so upsetting him. When he had collected Charlie earlier he had seemed his usual self.

'Look, Ellie, I must rush off and finish my packing. If you and Charlie want to go down and start breakfast don't wait for me. I have one or two calls I must make.' And she was left looking at the closed door, wondering what on earth had gone wrong.

Charlie was no help. While her mother wielded the hairdrier she chattered on. Ben had said and done this, Ben had said and done that, as if nothing of importance had ever happened in her life before. Ben had told her he had a pool in his house in California. 'It looks right over the ocean, Mummy, and sometimes you can see the whales gathering there at breeding times.'

'Lucky old Ben,' said Ellie, with more than a touch of sarcasm—which should have helped to relieve her feelings.

'Mummy, don't you like Ben?'

'Mmm. Yes, I like him. Why do you ask?'

'Just something in your voice. I thought maybe you didn't like him. But I like him more than anyone I've ever met—'cept for you. And Grandma.'

'I'm really glad of that.' Ellie pushed the drier back

into the holder. 'I should have been upset if you had said any different. But now I think we'll go down and have something to eat. We don't want to keep Ben waiting, do we?'

But they had almost finished eating by the time Ben came to join them. He sent Ellie one searing, accusing, bitter glance before he sat down and ordered.

'Have you finished your packing, Ben?' Such an effort to speak. There was so much about him now that was upsetting, almost intimidating.

'Yes.' Another look which she found puzzling. Moodiness was not something she would ever have associated with him and... Last night he had certainly given no sign of being ready to give up—the reverse, if anything. Of course, he had slept on it, as she had, and had perhaps reached the same conclusion. Her spirits sank a little. It was so unexpected. She had grown used to being pursued by this successful, attractive man, and it had lent her a glow, had done wonders for her ego, but...

But it was possible he was regretting the waste of so much valuable time and money. If he had been counting on a return then he was bound to look on the trip to Paris as a poor investment. That inescapable conclusion was surprisingly wounding, since it fitted in so perfectly with her own decision of the previous night.

'So—' she must be brisk, prevent her thoughts from dwelling on what was painful '—you'll want to be on the road as soon as possible, Ben. Come on, Charlie, you're all sticky with black cherry jam. A quick wash and we'll be back down by the time Ben has finished.'

During the journey it seemed to Ellie Ben's conversation was solely for Charlie, that she was for some mysterious reason being kept at arm's length, but it was as well she could not see into his mind, as she might have wished.

For Ben Congreve had, since that ill-advised last-minute dip in the hotel pool, been struggling with a ghastly suspicion, one which, should it be confirmed, would cast a devastating blight over the rest of his life. And, since his father would be involved, it could further undermine so many precious memories... His thoughts were bleak, devoid of hope, and he was afraid this morning had merely confirmed and clarified the vague, elusive anxiety which had persisted over the past few days.

They were in England and heading for Sussex sooner than seemed possible. Charlie had drowsed off and Ellie determined to be relaxed. 'What are your plans, Ben? Are you going back to the States immediately?'

'No.' His quick glance seared. 'There are one or two things I must clear up before I can do that.'

'I see.' Which was a lie. And there had been a powerful implication in his manner. Just as long as it did not involve her or Charlie—but that hope was soon extinguished.

'And I need your help.'

'Of course.' Her brain refused to work. 'I shall help you in any way I can, but...I'm not sure...'

'Let's leave it for now. It's impossible to have a serious discussion in a car.' His tone was curt, decisive, as if any thoughts she might have on the subject were of no importance. So she made no reply, simply sat simmering with rage, her face turned to the window. It was a great relief when she saw the turn-off for the village, and a moment later they were pulling up in front of the house.

The sound of gravel crunching beneath the wheels brought Charlie back to life. She released her seat belt with a cry of delight. 'Oh, good, we're home.'

Ben could find his usual teasing mood for Charlie, it seemed. 'And all the time I thought you were enjoying Paris and Disneyland.'

'Oh, I did, I did—' a not too serious show of embarrassment '—I didn't mean it like that, Ben. I just like being home too. But thank you.' Spontaneously she leaned forward, put her arms about his neck. 'Thank you, Ben, for the wonderfullest holiday of my life. It was brilliant and I can't wait to tell Linda about it.'

Suitcases and parcels were unloaded, and Ben, despite protests from Ellie, carried them upstairs to the bedrooms. The pleasure of the trip to Paris was beginning to slip to the back of her mind now. She was aware of the turmoil in her stomach and she was finding the tension between them almost too much to deal with, could not imagine what had caused it...

'May I use your telephone, Ellie?'

'Of course.' She waved him to where it stood on the hall table and meantime retreated to the kitchen, closing the door and reaching for the kettle. They had eaten nothing since breakfast and everyone must be hungry; she certainly was. And Wendy, bless her, expecting them back, had left French baguettes, with Brie, and there was fruit... The kitchen door opened and Ben, his face inscrutable, stood there.

'I've just rung the Red Cow. They can fit me in overnight.'

'Oh?' Colour came and went in her face. Emotions out of control. Joy at the prospect of delaying his departure a little longer, apprehension at the thought of the strain… 'I…you could have stayed here. I didn't think…'

'And spoil your spotless reputation?' A definite note of sarcasm and scorn. 'I would not dream of it.'

Her anger rose swiftly. If he could be cruel there was no need for her to shrink. Turning, she placed the plate of bread and cheese on the table. 'As to that, I'm afraid the damage is already done. Little Transome is extremely conservative. My reputation will be gone for ever now.'

'Oh, yes?'

'Oh, yes,' she repeated in an edgy voice. 'Yes. Respectable widows do not go off to Paris with famous writers and come back undamaged. Crazy, isn't it, Ben? I'm afraid I shall be judged severely regardless of any damage limitation exercise I can mount.'

Searching eyes on her face threatened to bring that humiliating slow burn out on her skin, and his next remark made her doubly glad she had been, for once, able to exert control. 'In that case it's a pity Charlie woke up last night.' The pause was long enough to allow her brain to switch on to his meaning, and he smiled grimly as the colour rose suddenly like a tide. 'I swear, if David—' he injected the name with a fair amount of dislike '—could see you now you would be found guilty with no fair trial. From my point of view an opportunity lost.'

There was no indication that the sudden and sharp deterioration in their relationship was affecting him as it was her, but perhaps that was because he was as used to hiding his deepest feelings as she was. It was bitter for him to recall that until this morning he had been convinced they were edging towards a close understanding.

It was a trend he'd been prepared to nurture carefully; he'd had no intention of jeopardising further progress by putting her under pressure. And, as a result, deep inside him was an ache—primitive, as old as time, he imagined, and completely novel for Ben Congreve.

It wasn't simply that from their first meeting he had known he had come to the end of a life-long search; he had decided that the best way to win her was to respect her previous relationship, no matter how jealous he might be of her husband, no matter how intense his own feelings, he would try to be patient.

But now he found himself resenting her almost as passionately as he had previously admired her, and for something so nebulous and insubstantial. But even suspecting her of deceit, imagining her to be less perfect than his previous idea of her, was enough to induce a cynical perspective. But she was answering his last, rather cheap observation…

'You missed no opportunity last night.' Her colour was fading, leaving her rather pale. 'Like most men, you think if you are persistent enough you will get your own way, but in this case you are quite wrong. The opportunity existed only in your mind. But if that is how you feel about it, let me put it this way…' She found herself on the verge of enjoying this opportunity; it was a salve for the terrible ache in her chest, a chance to hit back in a way which would damage his self-esteem. 'I realise you spent a great deal of money on us, and I hate the thought of being in your debt, so…' Ignoring his expression, she forced herself to go on, but with diminishing confidence. 'If you will give me some idea of what

I owe you, I really would prefer... I am fiercely independent, you see.'

'I shan't trouble to answer that.' He turned towards the door. 'But there is another reckoning to be done—nothing at all to do with money—and, as I said earlier, I shall want, demand, your help with that. I shall come back this evening, Ellie.'

She followed as he strode through the hall and towards the front door. 'But I was going to make coffee, and there's food...' Such a plaintive tone was idiotic in the circumstances.

'You and Charlie will enjoy it. Doubtless you will find it a relief to be on your own for a time.' At that moment Charlie came rushing down the stairs, then stood on the bottom step, swinging from the banister.

'Ben, you're not going, are you?'

'I'm going.' He mustered a faint smile, his whole matter softening. 'But, if I may, I'll come back this evening. Your mother and I have something to discuss and it would be a good idea if you were to go to bed early.'

'Oh? *Must* I, Mummy?' An appealing look towards Ellie.

'If you would—just this once, darling.' Crazy to be on the brink of tears. 'It would be such a help, and you've had a lovely time thanks to Ben...' Ignoring his cynical sideways glance, she turned with a formal hostessy smile. 'Well, if you refuse to stay to lunch, Ben, what time shall I expect you this evening?'

'I shall come as soon as possible after dinner.' And without another word, he opened the door.

They stood, the mother and child, listening to the car accelerating down the drive.

For the rest of the day Ellie determined to banish all

the worry from her mind, and the practicalities of life helped her to do that. There was the washing to be dealt with, and then she took a moment to look at some of the sketches which had been in her mind before Ben's whirlwind decision to whisk them off to Paris. But it was hard to resist the temptation to drift off into a dream in which all the problems between them were swept away; impossible for her to keep her mind on the task when her whole being was missing him to such an extent, when her body was crying out for the comfort of his.

A groan which tried to be self-mocking issued from her throat as she folded her arms on the table, laid her head on top and allowed a few tears to dampen the sleeves of her blouse. Part of her stratagem in going off with Ben in the first place was that in some perverse way she could punish him, but now she was fairly certain she had punished herself much more.

It wasn't so much that he had left her alone and pregnant—that was something she had come to terms with years ago—it was the fact that he had forgotten her existence, while she…she had had him indelibly etched on her memory. She had as much chance of forgetting him as of failing to recognise her reflection when she looked in a mirror, but that changed nothing.

She ached for him now as she had done right back at the beginning, and, OK, she had clung to the moral high ground, but that was no substitute for a man's arms about you, nor the touch of his mouth on yours. Virtue would be little comfort in the days ahead, when all she had were bitter memories.

'Mummy.' Charlie rushing into the room brought Ellie's head up with a jerk and her mind back to the present. 'You didn't hear the telephone, but I answered it for you and it was for me, really. Mum, Jane wants to know if I can go over for tea at her house and sleep there.'

'Oh, Charlie, you'll be too tired…'

'But it's a sleep-over, Mummy.' She gave a wail of protest at the prospect of exclusion from the latest fad to hit Little Transome. 'And Jane's mother will come and pick me up…and it won't be any trouble…and you'll be able to get on with some work…and you can talk to Ben and…'

There was no answer to all of that, and it was to an extent true. She *could* get on with some work between Charlie's departure and Ben's arrival.

After the flurry of goodbyes—more appropriate to a trip to the South Pole than a few hours' sleep-over— Ellie had time for a leisurely shower, and as she sat drying her hair afterwards she tried to keep her mind on work, to dismiss this persistent worry about Ben's motives. It was impossible to imagine what lay behind it all.

Damn it all. She rose from her drawing board in her work room. She *must* try to concentrate. All she had to do was decide whether to go ahead with a limited run of the new line she had designed. A limited edition of short lacy dresses, very glamorous and sophisticated. And expensive. That was the problem. Would anyone pay the price, which was bound to be high…?

With another groan, she threw off her satin housecoat, went to the cupboard and picked up the prototype from the rail. Knowing her own measurements to the millimetre, she always designed and tested her new ideas with herself in mind before making any commitment.

She took the cobwebby garment from its draped cotton cover, slipped it from its hanger and sighed with pleasure, reassured now that she had seen its perfection. It was so lovely she scarcely needed to try it on.

Nevertheless, she did, first taking a few minutes for a quick make-up—a touch of lipstick, a flick of mascara—and even a blast of her favourite Givenchy, all of which would enhance the final result. Then she slipped the delicate silk-lined garment over her shoulders, watching her reflection carefully. She twitched it down, adjusting the mid-thigh hemline. The back zip was as difficult as ever, but at last it slipped up. It caught on something at the nape of her neck so she didn't force it.

She took a step back from the long cheval mirror between the two floor-length windows in her bedroom and drew in a breath of admiration. Then, quickly turning away, she brought out some new black stockings, which she pulled on. Finally, a pair of black pumps, with medium heels, and she turned and walked towards her reflection.

Yes. Oh, yes. She had been right. Tomorrow she would give instructions for the girls to begin the first run. It was going to be a great success. The unusual lacy stitching, difficult and time-consuming for the knitters to execute but perfect, the whirling feathers in silver and black... Already she was planning variations: black with purple, black with nutmeg. And the fit was sheer perfection, except...

Ellie frowned. Was it possible she had put on a fraction of an inch here and there? The dress was certainly quite snug. A hand ran the length of her body, smoothing out the material... No, she didn't think so.

The length was unusual for her; she was more into

longer skirts. What was it Ben had said about all her friends being older? She wondered if that was what he'd meant. Certainly right now it seemed a pity to hide her legs when they were long and reasonably shapely. She was only twenty-seven, for heaven's sake, and they deserved an occasional airing.

The plain round neck looked good, and the tight elbow sleeves ending in that cheeky little flounce... All it needed was some jewellery—nothing very much, but the long silver earrings Wendy had brought back from Portugal last year... They would be perfect.

Next moment they were on, and she grinned at herself. For the moment her major problems were submerged in professional pride, and she bundled her hair on top of her head, turning this way and that to study the effect...

And then, outside, she heard the crunch of tyres on the gravel. She ran to the window in a panic, in time to see Ben stride up to the front door and to hear almost instantly the firm rat-tat of the knocker.

For a second or two she was paralysed. *Too early.* Her brain refused to admit what was happening, and then she was wrestling with a zipper which refused to budge. She paused for breath. The knocker was even more imperative, the zipper as firmly stuck. Then—horror—Ben had opened the door.

She could imagine him poking his head round before he called her name... It was time for her to decide... At least, there was no decision to be made. Quite simply she had a choice: to go down as she was or... No, she had no choice.

'I'm coming, Ben.' She straightened up, walked across the upper landing, put her hand on the mahogany banister and began a slow descent.

In the end it was all she could do—make the most of the situation and go down the staircase as if she were in some great house, putting on her first fashion show. How often had she dreamed of doing just that? But with Ben Congreve following her every move, her legs were much shakier than she would have dreamed. And if she had expected his eyes to grow cloudy with admiration she was disappointed. Certainly they never left her face, but it was cynicism she saw rather than anything else.

'Ben.' Her voice was entirely steady; that was good. 'You're early.'

His eyes were searching out her most private thoughts. 'And you want me to say I couldn't stay away a moment longer?'

A slap on the face, but she didn't flinch, merely raised her chin and produced a smile. 'No, I didn't expect you to say anything like that.'

'But so much effort, my dear.' A slow examination, head to toe and back, deliberately demeaning. 'And such a waste of time.'

'The "effort"—' she found a note of businesslike formality '—was not intended for you, Ben.'

'Ah…' It was as if her words carried some obscure but profound meaning. 'I see…'

'I doubt you do. But would you care for a drink?' She led the way into the sitting room, glad she had taken time to light the fire, which was blazing brightly, and waved him to a seat.

'No, not for me,' he said as she put a hand out for the decanter.

'Very well.' Taking a seat by the fire, she resisted an urge to pull wildly at her skirt. Her legs were looking good in the semi-opaque black, and so what? She crossed them negligently and lay back as if she were at ease. Which she wasn't—not with her heart hammering so urgently she thought he must see. After all, this wisp of a dress clung to every curve. 'You have some matter you wish to discuss with me, Ben?' Best to seize the initiative.

'Charlie is asleep?'

'Charlie has been invited to a sleep over with a friend.'

'Good.' A comment she chose to misunderstand, and her lips tightened disapprovingly at this slight to her child. His raised eyebrow said he had noticed, but there was no apology. 'It's best if there's no chance of us being disturbed. No point in hurting Charlie; she's done nothing to deserve it.'

'I gather what you are saying is that I do? Deserve to be hurt.' Pain rose inside her like a monster, making her voice shaky, but she refused to give in. While she had no idea what she was to be accused of, equally she had no intention of making it easy for him. But no matter what she had *thought* might be the charge against her, his next words had her reeling with shock.

'Tell me, Ellic.' He, too, seemed to be having difficulty expressing his feelings. There was something tortured about his manner, and the eyes on her face were bleak and unwinking. 'Did you and my father have a long and passionate affair?'

All the blood drained from her brain then. The room seemed to sway about her, and if she hadn't been sitting she was sure she would have fallen. 'I…' She frowned, trying to find his words in the jumble of her mind, then discarding them as being too fanciful. 'What?' A hand went up to her face and then dropped. 'Did I have...*what*?'

It was almost as if he were embarrassed—humiliated, perhaps. He rose, walked to the window and stood there, looking out, hands in the pockets of his pale grey trousers, a disconsolate aspect to him which made her ache in sympathy. Suddenly, as if summoning all his courage, he swung back to her. 'That's all I'm asking. I'd rather you told me, put me out of—' The words were bitten off, and he watched as she pushed herself from her seat and took a few steps across the room in his direction. 'What I suppose I'm asking is...is Charlie my half-sister?'

For what seemed like an hour, but was in reality a few seconds, she tried to unscramble the words in her mind. They made so little sense, and then...then they did, and on a rising tide of fury she raised her hand and with great deliberation she struck him with all her strength. 'How *dare* you—of all people?' Her voice shook so dangerously she could say no more. She whirled away, going to stand by the fireplace, one hand on the mantelpiece, her head drooping as she gazed blankly into the leaping flames. When she heard his step behind her, she spoke without looking, this time with sheer loathing as his accusation clarified. 'And now, please would you leave my house?'

'Yes. I shall do that. In a moment I shall do that, and then we need never see each other again if that is what you decide. But I must, for my own peace of mind, have an answer to my question, Ellie.'

'Your question was an insult to me as well as to your father.'

'You are avoiding the question.' His voice had hardened too, as if he were preparing to argue to the bitter end. 'Are you telling me you never knew my father?'

'You truly are unbelievable.' Now she found the strength to raise her head and glare at him. 'And I see no reason why I should answer such an impertinent question, but simply to bring a humiliating situation to an end, I shall tell you. As far as I am aware, I have never met your father. And if you are still unconvinced, then I suggest you ask him yourself.' The moment she spoke it occurred to her that while at one time, back in the past, his father's name had often cropped up in conversation, this time...

'That is something I cannot do, since he died last year.'

'Well, I'm sorry, but isn't it very disloyal of you to...?' It was all too much, too sordid. Tears stung and she was sure she was within a hair's breadth of total melt-down, but she would not give him the satisfaction of seeing her reduced to weeping. 'Now, if that's all, I'd like to be left alone.' She choked back a sob.

'Ellie.' He made as if to touch, to comfort, but when she recoiled as if fearing contamination, he stood watching as she sank down onto her chair. 'Ellie, forgive me. I'm causing you great pain, but you must know how I feel about you, and when I saw...at the pool this morning with Charlie...' The introduction of her daughter's name brought up Ellie's head with a jerk. 'Ellie, Charlie has a very distinctive birthmark on her buttock.'

'Yes.' She answered slowly, trying to tie this in with something he had said earlier, something her brain had refused to admit. 'Yes, she was born with a leaf-shaped mark at the top of her leg. Lots of children have these birthmarks but they are of little significance.'

'A mark in the shape of a tiny maple leaf.' His eyes were boring into hers and she nodded slightly. 'That mark has been distinctive in the Congreve family for several generations.' An endless pause. Her heart was beating in slow, mesmerising strokes, and she felt as if she were in thrall to a hypnotist, mind and body dissociated. 'My sister is marked with that identical naevus, and both her children.'

Still she stared, one part of her longing to throw the truth at him, the other unwilling to solve his problem. 'So?' She uttered in a cool tone, falsely dispassionate.

'So...' Another hardening of his manner. The words came through clenched teeth. as if he were hanging onto control with the utmost difficulty. 'What I am asking is, are you in some way related...to my family? It is very important to me to know.'

'Since I have assured you that your father and I never met—' her tone was off-hand, very nearly cruel; she wondered if she were finding some sadistic pleasure in his unhappiness '—I can't see where this interrogation is leading.'

'It seems so much of a coincidence... To meet you at Robert Van Tieg's, who was a contact of my father's, to feel for you as I did, and then...'

'Don't you think you're going slightly over the top? Coincidences occur all the time. I'm sure your novels are full of them.'

'We're talking about fact, not fiction.'

'My advice to you, Ben, is to leave it alone.' She knew she sounded patronising, that it didn't please him, but knew she had to carry on, to try to divert him. 'Even if you were to find out, it might not be the kind of information you would wish to have...'

'I wonder why you should say that, Ellie?' He pounced upon the words, which she immediately realised had been incautious. 'Why wouldn't I wish to have the information? If it concerns me—or, come to that, if it concerns you—then I want to know. In fact I have the right to know.'

'But we don't always, do we?' All at once she was feeling weak and defeated, exhausted by the years of cover-up and evasion, at the end of her tether, anxious to be rid of her problems once and for all. 'And as for you having the right to know my business, then I could hardly disagree more with your statement.'

'If, as I had begun to imagine, you and my father had had a relationship, then it would have had the most profound effect on my feelings for you. Or at least…'

'Really, Ben.' She knew she was losing it, and it hardly mattered any more. She rose, walked aimlessly about the room. 'I wish you would leave your father out of the equation entirely. If you have suspicions then maybe you should look closer to home—' Trying to bite off the last words, she failed, stood gazing at him.

Anguish was etched clearly on both their faces.

'Wh-what is that supposed to mean?' Then, as she shook her head, he strode towards her, grasped her shoulders tightly as if he would have liked to shake her. But then his manner softened. 'Tell me, Ellie. We can't go on like this. What did you mean?'

'For God's sake, can't you see it?' A touch of hysteria in the voice, in the eyes which flashed with a dangerous light. 'Or perhaps it's that you *won't* see it, that you still refuse to face up to—' She broke off, unable for the moment to go on.

'Ellie.' Ben was tight-lipped, determined, and she knew there was no place left for her to run.

'Charlie is your daughter. Yours and mine. And the tragedy is, you can't even remember how it happened.'

For all eternity they gazed at each other, until in the end his stricken face brought a sob to her throat. Another racking, painful sound betrayed her misery, and she was unable to resist the longing, the yearning. She laid her face against his chest; she allowed his arms to come round her in a protective gesture.

And his face coming to rest on the top of her head was a tiny balm for all the desolate years.

CHAPTER TEN

DEAR God! As Ben Congreve cradled the slender body against his, eyes closed, cheek resting against the sweetly scented hair, his mind struggled to deal with the enormity of what she had said.

It was impossible, and yet…knowing how he felt now, it was easy enough to understand how he could have been swept away by the same cataclysmic emotion he had been fighting ever since that first sight of her in Singapore. And there was that blank period in his life… The dates would be about right, but… But to have inflicted that on a young woman—any young woman— but especially this… And to have no memory of it. He wondered if he could ever forgive himself. Or could she?

Hard for Ellie to remember how long the storm of trembly misery had lasted, but, returning to some degree of awareness, she found herself on the sofa, Ben's arms still about her. He was comforting her with tiny hushing sounds, stroking with infinite gentleness. Then he was drying her face with a large handkerchief, apparently undiscouraged by the blotchy sight she must present.

'Ellie…' From his expression it was clear that he too was suffering deeply. The dark eyes were shadowy, somber, with none of the illuminating pleasure they so often showed when he looked at her. Now he was grave, very nearly desolate. 'Do you feel like talking?'

She didn't, but, knowing she must, nodded, shrugging

her shoulders in a dazed kind of fashion. 'Ben…I hardly know where to start.'

'Before we go on—' detaching himself slightly, he sat back and examined her closely '—is there anything I can get you? Tea scarcely seems to fit the situation…' He saw her shake her head and then went on. 'Can I say something before you tell me your story?'

'Yes.' A postponement would be welcome, would give her time to get her voice under control. She had never been weepy and could hardly understand why she had broken down now, except…there had been such a build-up of stress and pressure.

'That very first day—the first moment, in fact, when I saw you at the Van Tiegs'—I…'

'You mentioned Robert in connection with your father. I can't see…'

'Shh,' he persuaded her. 'We'll come to all that in time. I just want you to know, from the moment I saw you, I knew I had found something special. I didn't know how, I just knew I had to find out more about you. Something said you were going to be very important in my life. And when I knew you were a widow, I couldn't resist the temptation to find myself passing your door one day, to drop in…'

Her smile, wan and wistful, reflected her physical and emotional exhaustion. 'I thought that story was too much of a coincidence.'

'You were right to be suspicious. But still, I was determined not to rush you. I knew I had to curb my impatience—not easy for a man like me—but I sensed this was to be the most important thing in my life, and I wasn't going to spoil things by rushing. I was prepared to use your daughter as a means of drawing closer, and that worked to a certain extent. Don't get me wrong, Charlie is a sweetie, and if what you say is true…'

'Do you doubt it?' She was filled with passionate indignation. 'How could I concoct such a story?'

'No, I know you wouldn't. Of course I know. Forgive me, Ellie, it's simply so much to take in at once. And, as you said earlier, my tragedy is that I don't remember. At least… I have been aware of something, something powerful pulling me towards you, but that I put down to this overwhelming attraction. Something I've never experienced for any other woman in my life before.'

Tenderness, guilt, sorrow flooded him as he looked at the downcast features, the long lashes describing tiny fans on her cheeks. 'Or, at least, God help me, I cannot remember it. I imagine we must have met in the Windwards?'

'Yes.' A heartfelt sigh. 'At least you remember being there.'

'No, I don't remember it, but I know I was there at the right time. In fact, it's something I can't explain, but I always had this strong urge to go back—looking for something, as I have been ever since the accident.'

'The accident?' Her head jerked back sharply, wide eyes raking his features as she tried to pick up some clues.

'I was in a sailing accident. You would know I was setting off for the Galapagos, and we were struck by a typhoon. Dan—did you know him?' She nodded and he went on. 'Dan was apparently washed overboard. I never saw him again, and it seems I was struck when the mast snapped off. But it's all supposition. In any case, eventually the boat was taken in tow to Chile. I was in a coma there for several weeks before eventually I was well enough to be flown home to the States. But my memory of the time immediately before the accident is simply wiped out. Physically, I made a complete recovery, but that part has always been an elusive blank. From time to time there's an odd flash of recollection, but it's gone before I can catch hold of it.'

'My God.' Misery, sheer anguish stabbed at her. 'And all those years…' Fiercely she bit on her lower lip, determined to exert iron control on her emotions. 'All that time waiting for a call, and you… So many wasted years.'

'Not wasted, Ellie.' Reaching out, he took her hands, taking them first to his lips, then holding them against his chest. 'Not wasted when you've done such a wonderful job with Charlie. I'm the one who's wasted so many long years.'

'Your marriage?'

'Yes. My marriage. When I got back home I found I had a ready-made fiancée. The wedding was in hand and I allowed myself to drift along with it. I had an elusive memory of some of it, but still, I knew something wasn't quite right. I had this vague notion of the girl I was going to marry. She had a halo of blonde curls and…' Hearing her exclaim, he stopped, waited, then, as she said nothing, he went on, 'And although Debbie was—is—blonde, she didn't quite fit the picture.'

'At the time we met I'd had my hair coloured—blonde. And cut so it curled all over my head.'

'But why, Ellie? For heaven's sake why didn't you get in touch? I had a right to know. Nothing on this earth would have kept me from you. And to think of you alone, pregnant…'

'I did try. Believe me. I had a friend who had contacts.

He found out your telephone number but when I did call, I spoke to a servant. She told me none of the family was available and that you were being married the next day. After that there seemed little point. I had met Greg and…'

'Oh, God.' He put his head in his hands, raking his fingers through his hair. 'Are you telling me you married simply to avoid being a single mother?'

Recalling the anguish made her speak like an automaton. 'I married to protect my parents from worry and shame. Dad was a retired diplomat. He was about to take up a very high-profile position with a Japanese company. I knew they would have hated it, but…of course they guessed. And by then it was too late.'

'And…the man you married?'

'The man who married me, you mean. Out of sheer kindness. I met Greg Osborne shortly after I arrived in London. I rented a bedsit in his house and when he found out about…about Charlie, he decided I should be his housekeeper and that led on to marriage. He knew he had very little time to live and, since he had no relatives, no one else would be involved. I think for the last few months he was happier, certainly more comfortable, than he had been since his sister died some years before. It's as simple as that. But I would not have agreed if I hadn't liked him so much. He had a great sense of humour, and he made me laugh when I didn't have a lot to laugh about. I never had any regrets about accepting his generous offer.'

'And when he died?'

'When he died, I was left with his house in Pimlico. I mourned him as a father figure—he was much older than I was, and much wiser too. It was he who first started me off in knitting. He had an old machine his sister had used; he dragged it down from the attic one day and got it back into working order. Without him I doubt if I would have thought of starting my own business.

'But after Charlie was born I was desperate to get out of the city. I sold the house and had just enough to pay a deposit on this one. It was very run-down, but then gradually, as money started to come in, I had all the improvements done which had been in my mind when I first saw it. And it's all been a great success. I have so much to thank Greg for—his name, the house and the business. All down to him.'

'You're brilliant. Do you know that?' For the first time that evening his eyes held hints of laughter, and Ellie felt some of the ache ease from her soul. 'A brilliant mother, a successful businesswoman and...'

'And you're brilliant too. At least, so I'm told.' The mischievous tone was a surprise to Ellie herself, even if her voice was unsteady... 'A brilliant writer, according to Tanya, who knows about these things.'

'Ouch.' A tiny grimace. 'Are you determined to cut me down to size?'

'I'm not.'

'You would have every right.' As he leaned forward his face grew more serious. He traced the line of her mouth with a forefinger. 'Even though I can remember nothing about it, I find it hard to forgive myself for leaving you to face what you did. How could I have been so damned careless? I've always thought of myself as responsible, and yet...'

'Don't.' It was painful for her to listen, and there was no way she could allow him to shoulder all the responsibility. 'Don't, Ben. It wasn't entirely your fault. In fact…' Averting her face, she had to force herself to keep talking. 'It wasn't your fault at all, for you did ask me. Admittedly—' a deep blush '—you didn't ask until things had reached…well, the point of no return, but I…I gave you to understand there was no risk. So you see, I needed no persuasion to rush into an affair.'

'And I sailed away with no thought…'

'That's what it seemed like. I had given you my parents' number and I waited for you to make contact, even though by then I had heard you had a fiancée waiting for you back in the States.'

'I'm beginning to understand your attitude when we met up in Singapore.' He sighed deeply. 'The picture you paint is not a very pretty one—selfish, self-indulgent, and…'

'I never thought along those lines, and in any case, you could have had no idea about…about Charlie. And we were behaving much as everyone else did at that time. If there was carelessness then it was down to me, though it took me some time to admit as much. But in the end I did face up to it, and by the time Charlie arrived I had no regrets. But…' She paused, searching his face. 'Your father, Ben? What part does he play in all this?'

'My father? Well, when he died I found he'd had another woman in England. We never found out her name, but when I saw the Congreve mark on Charlie's leg, then… My brain went into overdrive, putting two and two together and coming up with the wrong answers. As I said, it was only after Dad died we knew. There were references among his papers about their meetings and it seemed to be someone he had met through Robert Van

Tieg. I jumped to the conclusion that it was you. I wasn't thinking straight, but it would have explained your coolness, your reluctance to become involved—of course it would be embarrassing for you to be pursued by your lover's son…'

'But that was the first time I had met Robert. It was Jenny I knew.'

'Well, as I said, I wasn't thinking rationally, and I was jealous as hell. If you *had* had an affair with Dad that meant the end of any hopes I had. I could never have you. It would have seemed…I could never have shared you with him.'

'In fact, Ben, you've never shared me with anyone.' The words were out before she had time to consider, but it seemed an appropriate time to let him know that important fact.

'I see.' For a long time he looked at her. 'Not even Greg?'

She shook her head, all the fine tresses of hair flying about her face, taking up golden shafts of light from fire and lamplight. 'Especially not Greg.' Later she might explain in more detail.

'So…as well as everything else, I've deprived you of any kind of normal relationship.'

'Not exactly.'

'Not exactly?' A raised, questioning eyebrow. 'I wonder what that means?'

'It means I wasn't deprived because I was never in the least tempted.'

A faint smile now, the lips curving pleasurably upwards. Again a finger came out to brush against her mouth, a surprisingly intoxicating gesture as her increased heartbeat was confirming. 'So…' His eyes, too, gave the impression of concentrating on her mouth while his fingers held steady her chin. 'All those hours of jealousy over David Merriman were just pointless negative emotions?'

'Not quite.' Obeying an impulse, one of the many things she was recalling from her time spent in the South Seas, she twisted her legs beneath her, knelt on the sofa and leaned towards him. 'At least not from my point of view. I'm very glad you were jealous.'

The sparkle in his eyes told her he was enjoying the battle of words. 'But that first night here, when I was the man who came to dinner. You went out of your way to give the impression that you and David were an item. Confess.'

'Maybe,' she admitted, knowing he had hit the nail on the head. 'But surely you can see that was because I saw you as a threat? I was afraid of my own reaction to you. And I also had a very guilty secret which at all costs I had to keep from you. And, as well, I knew that if I became involved with you again, I would be hurt again. It was something I could hardly bear to risk.'

'But you knew I was divorced.'

'Yes.' She wriggled, made slightly uncomfortable by his close observation. 'It was easier to convince myself that you might have let your wife down as you had me. And besides, I knew I would find it difficult—impossible, even—to keep you at arm's length…'

'So you were using the doctor as a Rottweiler?' Such an unlikely comparison brought a reluctant giggle, but before she could protest, he went on. 'And would you like to know the real reason why Debbie and I divorced?'

'Only if you want to tell me.'

'Well, first of all, we weren't really compatible. Always in my mind there was a memory, edging her out, keeping us apart, but...the real reason was that she refused to have children, and I think they are an integral part of marriage and of life.'

'Oh?' Was this an accusation? Did he blame her for depriving him of his daughter's childhood, or...?

'Now, don't go imagining I'm blaming you for anything. How could I possibly justify such an attitude? Ellie, you must believe me.' Seeing her faint, indulgent smile, he went on. 'To tell the truth, I can't imagine how Debbie and I ever felt the urge to marry, except...our families were very close, and from the outsider's viewpoint it looked like an ideal match. And besides, she was—she is—very pretty.'

Ridiculous for Ellie to feel such a shaft of jealousy.

'But somehow, from the first, I was aware of something wrong, something missing from our relationship. In the end she met someone who could give her the kind of life she really wanted. She's a very gregarious creature; she loves being constantly surrounded by her friends. And now she's married to a man who shares her tastes, I'm confident she'll be happier. It was a very civilised divorce,' he added drily.

After a moment's contemplation he continued. And in such a softly persuasive voice she felt all her emotions, all her fragile hopes come together in an excess of longing. 'What I still can't understand is how I could have forgotten so completely almost everything about you, and yet...' a finger skimmed her cheek '...yet feel such instant recognition.'

'As to that...' her voice, her manner were dreamy, partly with reminiscence but mostly with this yearning need she felt for him '…I've told you. I had dyed my hair—it was a wholly different and quite unsuitable colour—and even my name was different. Then I was Helen Tenby. It was Greg who first called me Ellie and it stuck. And don't forget—' a more sober, realistic note crept into her voice '—we were together for just two weeks. So it's hardly surprising that you didn't remember.'

'Just two weeks? And with such devastating results.' He shook his head in disbelief. 'But you?' he said softly. 'Did you remember me? As you say, after so many years, did you even *want* to remember?'

'I knew you at once. At least…it was your voice. It raised the hairs on my scalp even before I could see your face. And don't forget you had changed quite a bit too.'

'Tell me?' White teeth flashed a brief smile. 'How have I changed?'

'Well, for one thing the beard has gone, and for another you were wearing some clothes.'

'You are shocking me, Miss Tenby that was.' Now he was close. She could feel his breath on her cheek, knew if she were to move her head the slightest degree their mouths would collide. But this was something she decided against. This tantalising moment was to be savoured, prolonged, and for once she was finding pleasure in the excited throb of her heart against her ribs.

But then, when he took the initiative, it was sheer bliss to capitulate, to allow him to turn her mouth to his, to push her back against the pile of cushions, capturing her hands and holding them above her head. Sheer bliss to contemplate what was to come.

She thought he spoke her name, but she was so wrapped up in a yearning sigh she wondered if it was her heightened imagination. And there was a sound in her own throat, a mix of such pleasure and longing. It was so delicious, this tormenting butterfly touch of his mouth against hers, so subtly teasing she could have cried out with the frustration of it, such sweet madness. Then one wrist was freed from his circling fingers and she found the back of his head, brought his mouth into such positive joyous contact with hers, wishing it would never end.

'Ellie, Ellie.' It was a long time before he spoke, and then it was to share his wonder with her, to demonstrate the same aching longings. 'My darling.' And the fingers brushing hair back from her forehead made her skin prickle with tender delight. 'What are we going to do?'

Drugged by her senses, she shook her head, unable to think of an answer, her mind just toying with the implication of such a question. 'I don't know. Does it matter? All I want is to stay like this. For ever.' And, to demonstrate, she brought his head down to hers again, surveying him wickedly, wantonly through half closed eyelids, began again the teasing delights of touch and withdrawal which caused such havoc with her senses. And his. 'For ever,' she repeated with a tortured sigh. Then she gasped as his hands slid beneath her, raising her body into the curve of his.

'I agree.' The trail of kisses the length of her cheek slowed as he reached the corner of her mouth. 'Nothing would give me more pleasure, but...but before things get out of control, perhaps it would be better to make it legal. First.'

Something about the word made her break off, frustrating this urgent desire she had to explore the contours of his body through the silk shirt. 'Legal?' The word might have been Swahili for all the sense it made to her.

'I mean to marry you—have done since that night at Robert's, and before that, I imagine, when we met in the Windwards.'

'You said nothing about it then.' The accusation slipped out before she could stop it.

'I think that would have been some kind of scruple. I must have realised I'd got myself into a mess, falling madly in love with one girl while back home... You know I have no recollection of that. I hope I thought the decent thing would be to break it off with Debbie before taking a wife...'

'If you say so,' she said demurely.

'And I'm waiting for an answer to my question.'

'Which was?'

'Which was a proposal of marriage, as you know.'

'Oh, I thought it was a declaration rather than a question, but...' A fear struck her, not entirely genuine, one she longed for him to dismiss. 'Do you think it wise to rush into it, Ben? After all, we've known each other for such a short time.'

'For more than seven years, I thought.'

'You know what I mean. Wouldn't it be ghastly if we made a mistake?'

'You think it might end up like that?'

'No, but I should hate to mess up your life again.'

'You didn't mess it up the first time. And the only way you'll do it again—' he grinned at the contradiction '—is if you refuse to marry me.'

'You know what I mean. And there's Charlie to consider.'

'Charlie and I are already great pals. We can break it to her later that I am in fact her father.'

'Your family will be awfully scandalised.'

'I doubt that very much. And if they are, then they will have to live with it. But they won't, I promise. My mother will be thrilled, and Amy too. And, incidentally, my mother knows nothing about Dad's involvement with someone else. With luck she need never know. It was something Amy and I found when we were dealing with some papers he kept in a personal file in his office. I'm sorry I even mentioned it to you, but, I admit, I was in a state of shock, and then there was your connection with Robert. The fact that Charlie could possibly be my half-sister... It was something I couldn't cope with—and any other explanation, especially the real one, did not occur to me.

'But now...' He paused, looking down at her with that peculiar expression, as if she were a rare and exotic gift, an expression which brought such a suffusion of tenderness and passion that she no longer had the slightest doubt about what she meant to do. 'Now...' It was a vague promise which required no further explanation except the lingering kiss which followed.

'And you do know...' Being so provocative was an additional and unexpected delight to her. 'You do know you caught me at a disadvantage by arriving earlier than I had expected.' She detached herself and stood up, smoothing the short dress down over her thighs while he watched, a slightly bemused expression on his face. 'And you caught me wearing one of my most dazzling creations.'

'I did notice,' he said drily. 'I thought you understood that.' It was a reminder of his earlier, slightly sarcastic remark. 'But what I meant to say was that you look stunning.'

'I had simply been trying it on but couldn't get out

of it when I heard the car. I knew it was not the most suitable garment for what I imagined was to be more a confrontation rather than a visit.'

'When I saw you...I had the idea you were planning seduction.'

'I was checking out this dress,' she began in a tone of indignation, 'which is due to go into production on Monday, and I found the zip had jammed. So—' she turned her back and held up the swathe of tawny hair '—would you please see if you can move it?'

With disconcerting ease he had it working, and she half turned, his hands at the same time reaching out for her again.

'Thank you.' Her face was pink.

'You expect me to believe that story?' The low throb in his voice found a response in the base of her stomach. 'And when you're wearing that very guilty look?'

'It is the truth.' But, to herself, she admitted it had a hollow ring.

'And you swear you had no thought of seduction?' Suddenly he swung her round to face him, his eyes searching her face mischievously.

'No.' Now her blush was furious. 'Not then.' And she stopped abruptly, after a moment smiling at her naïveté.

'But now?' His fingers were tracing a path the length of her spine, assuring himself that she wore nothing underneath, and then the palms of his hands were against the silky skin, arousing feelings which were a torture and a delight, emotions she had almost forgotten.

'Ah, now...' Now she was powerless, at the mercy of this potent throbbing build-up of pressure and excitement, this hyper-sensitivity of mind and body, such heady awareness...

'You remember what I said…?' How could she re-member anything when he was dropping a series of tiny butterfly kisses along the curve of her cheek? How could he *expect* her to remember anything when he moved before she could turn her head and intercept his mouth? 'I said, this time we should make it legal first.'

'*You* said,' the confirmation was followed by a plain-tive little moan, her head dropping against his shoulder so her words were very nearly muffled. 'I don't think my opinion was even sought.'

'So…' As he spoke he was leading her from the room. They were crossing the hall, climbing one slow step at a time up the shallow curving staircase. 'So…' another drugging kiss '…this time I'm prepared to concede.'

In the bedroom, the touch of a button brought heavy curtains swishing across the windows, enclosing them in a cocoon, softly lit by the glow of a single lamp. His hands were clasped loosely about her waist, her upturned face was intent on his, the wonderful, luminous eyes brilliant with longing. 'Ben.' His name came from her lips with a sigh, a note of pleading, and a shudder racked her as his hand came up to touch her face.

Then, when he moved to brush the delicate garment from her shoulders, she held her breath, noticing nothing but his reaction and hers when it fell away to land in a pool by her feet.

Impatience now, as his jacket landed on a chair, closely followed by shirt and tie, and they indulged in the inexpressible delight of tracing paths with fingertips across delicate skin. She rejoiced in the taste of him when mouths followed, and when her legs grew simply too weak to hold her she gloried in his strength, which held her close to him while he kissed the length of her throat before allowing her to subside onto the bed, pulling him down beside her.

'Ellie—' There was a break in his voice as he lay for a moment beside her, doing little but touching, bringing her to a pitch of fevered joy from which she never wanted to escape. 'My darling, this time, *this time* it will be for ever.'

And the time for words was past. Now all that mattered in her life was feeling—and how could she have forgotten that a man's body could be so silky and so tempting? Mouths met and parted, met again, while he whispered all kinds of delicious nonsenses which brought the most irresistible ripples of pleasure deep in the lower part of her stomach.

Another change of gear, and one hand circled the slender column of her neck, the other slid down over her hips, hitching her more closely into the curve of his body. All sense of time and space left her mind as he began that onslaught on her senses which took her to a quivering, breathtaking summit, held her there for a brief eternity before allowing her, in the security of his arms, to drift, still in a state of semi-enchantment, back to earth.

CHAPTER ELEVEN

WHEN Ellie woke there was a strange sensation. A hand, certainly not her own, lay against her naked stomach, and if she moved the merest inch she encountered... A quick indrawn breath, then a slow, relaxed exhalation as memory flooded back and she turned to Ben, hands reaching out, heart beating in wild agitation. Sleepily his eyes opened and he smiled, arms pulling her into him, and when he spoke his voice was slow, dreamy.

'You know, when people in years to come ask about the happiest day of my life, of course I shall say the day I married you. But we shall know, you and I, that in fact it was this day.' His hand reached out to the back of her head, inclining her mouth towards his.

'Ellie.' He spoke her name with such sensual, burning intensity, at the same time brushing her lips, once, twice, in unbearable teasing movements. And it was little wonder that her senses were again spiralling out of control, that she had neither the will nor the inclination to stop them. Nothing in the world was of any account except the perfection of this moment.

It was less than three weeks later that Ellie nervously waited in a bedroom of an exclusive London hotel. A moment earlier Wendy had taken an over-excited Charlie downstairs to check the reception room, to see that the flowers still looked perfect, that all of the guests were assembled. All that remained was for the bridegroom to arrive. Not that she had the slightest doubt, but it was strange… His last call had been most mysterious, and…

Suddenly the telephone shrilled. She rushed to pick it up, sighed with relief when she heard his voice.

'Darling. Where on earth have you been?'

'I'll explain it all later, but right now I'm about twenty yards away from you and have just had a shower. I'll meet you downstairs in about ten minutes—and, by the way, I love you.'

'And I love you.' It didn't matter that she was speaking to herself. She replaced the receiver, walked to one of the large mirrors and looked at her appearance as if she were studying it for the first time.

Although she had had some initial doubts, now she was glad she had broken with the tradition of wearing white—after all, it wasn't as if… But in any case, she liked this so much more: the cream satin skirt, narrow with just a hint of fullness at the back, ankle-length and elegant, and the snug little top in dark green velvet, which a scooped neckline trimmed with heavy cream guipure lace, the nipped-in waist which did wondrous things for her figure, and short sleeves. It was all so perfect for the informal wedding they had decided on. And with Charlie, the sole attendant, in a long dress of green velvet, it all looked very pretty…

'Mummy, Mummy, we've seen Ben and you'll never guess…'

'Charlie…' Wendy, who had followed her charge into the bedroom, spoke with a warning note which resulted in the child covering her mouth with her hand and giggling. 'Sorry. I forgot. It's a surprise. The bestest surprise ever, and—'

'Charlie.' Wendy, both exasperated and amused, shook her head. 'What are we going to do with you?'

'You saw Ben?' That was all Ellie could think of, her only interest right now.

'Yes, and he's gone down—and, oh, Mummy, I think we ought to *hurry*.'

'All right.' Her troubles all appeared to be ebbing away. In just a little time she was going to be Mrs Ben Congreve and there was nothing in the world she wanted more. And soon, soon, Charlie would be told the truth about her birth. Certainly there remained the problem of her business, but Ben had said they could live in England until she had made up her mind about that...and that would resolve itself as time went by.

'Ready, then?' She handed her daughter the small posy of cream roses and stephanotis, picked up her own and they walked across the hall to the elevator.

Ellie looked up from her daydream as they stopped on the next landing. 'Aren't we going right down?'

'This is the surprise, Mummy.' Charlie took her hand and began to pull.

'Wendy?' A puzzled look towards her friend, who nodded.

'Go on, Ellie, and meet your surprise. I'll see you downstairs.'

With total confidence Charlie led her mother a few steps along the corridor, then pushed open a door into a small hallway leading into a bedroom which for a moment seemed to Ellie to be crowded with people.

The first face she recognised, and with total surprise, was Jenny Seow, for she had understood that professional commitments would not allow... But here she was, smiling, stunning as ever in a dark kingfisher-blue cheongsam, and with Robert standing beside her.

Ellie's mouth was opening to express her pleasure when in some miraculous way they stood aside and revealed... The room seemed for a moment to sway, tears started to her eyes and she dropped to her knees on the carpet, oblivious of any damage to her cream satin.

'Mother. Oh, Mother.' She leaned with one hand on the arm of the wheelchair, laid her cheek against her mother's. 'Oh, what a truly perfect surprise.' From Jenny she took the tissue being offered and dabbed at her eyes, then with a giggle performed the same service for her mother. 'I just can't believe it.'

'Helen.' For a moment her mother held her close. 'I missed one wedding—do you really think I would have missed your second?'

'Oh, Mother!'

'Wasn't it a wonderful surprise?' Charlie was dancing from one foot to the other. 'And Ben arranged it all.'

'Ben?' A wondering look from Ellie.

'Yes,' her mother confirmed. 'That wonderful man you're about to marry. He arranged everything in collusion with Jenny and Robert. You see, these kind people sent a private plane for me. I stayed in the lap of luxury with them in Singapore and then we all came together. Cutting it pretty fine, I admit, but here we are. Oh, and this is Marti.' She indicated the woman who was standing behind the wheelchair. 'She's my nurse for the duration of my visit.'

'And now,' Jenny said, glancing at her watch, 'I think we had better go down. Otherwise poor Ben will think the bride has changed her mind.' Naturally, the irony of her remark escaped her. 'Robert, will you wait with Ellie and Charlie while we go downstairs? Don't be late, now.' And she left, with the nurse and Lady Tenby.

'So, Robert.' Ellie glanced at herself in a mirror, deciding her make-up had survived the emotional reunion. 'Are you having to give me away as well as everything else?'

'I have a list of orders from Ben—long as your arm. He's determined to make things perfect for you.'

'And I think he has succeeded. Thank you, Robert, for all you have done.' She sniffed, pressed a finger against her nose. 'I refuse to cry again. Ben might change his mind if I arrive all weepy and with a red nose.'

'Ben knows he's a very lucky man. You look beautiful—both of you.' He grinned down at Charlie. 'Not many men get two for the price of one.'

'Oh, *Robert*.' Charlie blushed, fluttering her lashes wildly.

A moment later they were all in the elevator which would take them down to the hotel chapel.

And there he was, in a tiny candlelit church, tall, wide-shouldered, hair still damp from the shower. As Ellie walked with Robert the length of the rich blue carpet her heart swelled with love. Her mind was a blur of joy and thanksgiving that life had held for her this supreme, this magical gift. And she blessed all the good fairies who had ever lived that they had brought her at last to this man, that there would be no more cruel separation.

They had reached him. Robert slipped away and Ben turned, dark eyes gleaming with mischief as he correctly interpreted her startled expression. White teeth against a dark silky beard—less full than it had once been, but these things could not be hurried—made her catch her breath. She looked into that same teasing, seductive expression which had caused such havoc to her emotions seven years before. He held out his hand and she placed hers in it, rejoicing in his strength as fingers linked. Then they turned to the clergyman, who was waiting so patiently.

Next morning, Ellie woke beside Ben in that same hotel in Paris—the one which would for evermore be known to them as 'our hotel'. But this time they were alone. Charlie had gone back to Little Transome with her grandmother, Wendy and Marti.

'Ben...' Since she spoke to herself it was a mere whisper, the simple pleasure of repeating his name. She would not disturb him, and yet...impossible to resist a finger against the silky beard—specially grown, he had told her, to remind her of the pirate she had fallen in love with. As if she needed reminding. 'Ben...' The silky brush against her skin evoked a treacherous throb deep down. 'I can never thank you enough...'

'Mmm?' With lazy, smiling satisfaction, he stirred, a foot reaching out to hook her closer at the same time as an arm curled about her waist. 'For what?' A drowsy, complacent question. 'If you mean what happened an hour or so ago...believe me, I enjoyed it at least as much—'

'I didn't mean *that*.' Which was not wholly truthful. 'At least—' a blush, a tiny movement took her deeper in the bed '—not *only* that. And you know it.' Determined to sound disapproving, she spoiled the effect with a giggle.

'You surprise me, since it's all that's on my mind at

the moment. So…' He adjusted his weight and position, pulling her into closer contact, and the brush of chest hair against delicate skin caused her to catch her breath. 'If not *that*, then what?' His mouth was against her cheek. 'And,' he said, with a muffled pleasured groan of mock protest, 'what form are your thanks to take?'

'I was thanking you like this—' a kiss, lips parted '—and this, for making our wedding so perfect. All those complex arrangements for bringing my mother over, and…'

'Well, I'm sure everyone who knew the real story would agree I owe you a wedding. And, if I made it perfect for you, then no other thanks are needed.'

'You know…' She hesitated, then went on, 'When we go to Sydney for Christmas as planned…'

'Mmm?' Idly, tormentingly, his fingers moved across her skin. She shuddered, caught at them and spoke with her mouth against his.

'When we reach Sydney, I'm going to tell Mother the whole truth.'

'Mmm.' Now that drowsiness was gone; he was wholly alert. 'If you're sure…only…'

'You don't think it's a good idea?'

'My only reservation is, she and I have this very satisfactory mutual admiration society going. I hope an outbreak of truth isn't going to alter her perception of me.'

'I shall make sure that does not happen.' A brush of her mouth against his. 'Already she thinks you're the son-in-law *sans pareil*.'

'But that's the risk, isn't it? From perfect son-in-law to vile seducer in one swift move. Perhaps you could let her down lightly, tell her I was putty in your hands— which is no more than the truth.'

'My mother knows too much about men ever to buy that one, but…I shall certainly let her know it was at least my fault too.'

'And, don't forget, we have another reception waiting when we reach the States. My mother will be in her element, arranging a party to welcome you and Charlie to…'

'I hope it isn't going to be too much for Charlie. Already she's on cloud nine.'

'Charlie will take it all in her stride. And since we're taking Wendy with us… Mmm…' He sniffed appreciatively. 'You smell delicious and I…'

'You know…David Merriman…?

'What?' His eyes flew open and he drew back reproachfully. 'What did you say? *This* is our honeymoon.'

'You can't still be jealous?' But it was impossible to ignore that slight feeling of satisfaction, that certain smug complacency.

'I can. Quite easily.'

'You have absolutely no need.'

'Well, as I told you before, your relationship with him was very damaging to my self-esteem, and it will take time…'

'What nonsense,' she said primly. 'And I won't have you translating a friendship into a relationship. You know I've had a relationship with one man only.'

'Mmm. Well, go on.' He sounded weary. 'If you must bring up the subject of the saintly doctor at this early stage…'

'I was about to say—and I heard this from Tanya some time ago—David does have another woman-friend. Someone nearer his own age,' she added innocently. 'So no one can disapprove. And I was also going to say, I don't think his heart will be broken over our marriage.'

'I am so relieved.'

'Don't be patronising. In any case, this older woman will be a very suitable wife. She is a sister in an Oxford hospital.'

'Mmm. Perfect. They'll be able to discuss bunions and glue ear over breakfast.'

'Now you're being mean.'

'No,' he laughed. 'I'm genuinely sorry for the guy. Having to settle for someone other than you...but tell me, are you beginning to feel hungry? You are? Then isn't it time we got up and dressed and went to find something to eat?'

'All right.' Ellie threw back the covers. 'What do you think I should wear, Ben?'

But before she could swing her legs out of the bed, Ben had caught hold of her hand. He raised it to his lips and with his eyes intent on hers began to feather kisses along the tender skin of her inner wrist. 'Let me say first of all that I much prefer you as you are now...'

'What?' She frowned, her eyes searching his face for some clue. 'What do you mean?'

'You asked me what you should wear and I'm expressing a preference. That's all.'

'Ben. Try to be serious.'

'Very well. I mean to please you in all things. But before we get up, there is another matter of great importance which demands your presence and your full attention.'

'Oh, yes?' Her eyes gleamed as she lay back on the pillows with a submissive little sigh, linking her fingers about his neck.

'Oh, *yes*,' he promised, and he was looking down at her with that dreamy threatening glint which promised such delight. 'Oh, yes.' And the dark piratical face blotted out the world.

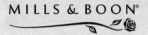

MILLS & BOON®

Next Month's Romances

Each month you can choose from a wide variety of romance novels from Mills & Boon®. Below are the new titles to look out for next month from the Presents™ and Enchanted™ series.

Presents™

JOINED BY MARRIAGE	Carole Mortimer
THE MARRIAGE SURRENDER	Michelle Reid
FORBIDDEN PLEASURE	Robyn Donald
IN BED WITH A STRANGER	Lindsay Armstrong
A HUSBAND'S PRICE	Diana Hamilton
GIRL TROUBLE	Sandra Field
DANTE'S TWINS	Catherine Spencer
SUMMER SEDUCTION	Daphne Clair

Enchanted™

NANNY BY CHANCE	Betty Neels
GABRIEL'S MISSION	Margaret Way
THE TWENTY-FOUR-HOUR BRIDE	Day Leclaire
THE DADDY TRAP	Leigh Michaels
BIRTHDAY BRIDE	Jessica Hart
THE PRINCESS AND THE PLAYBOY	Valerie Parv
WANTED: PERFECT PARTNER	Debbie Macomber
SHOWDOWN!	Ruth Jean Dale

On sale from 13th July 1998

H1 9806

Available at most branches of
WH Smith, John Menzies, Martins, Tesco,
Asda, Volume One, Sainsbury and Safeway

SPOT THE DIFFERENCE

Spot all ten differences between the two pictures featured below and you could win a year's supply of Mills & Boon® books—FREE! When you're finished, simply complete the coupon overleaf and send it to us by 31st December 1998. The first five correct entries will each win a year's subscription to the Mills & Boon series of their choice. What could be easier?

Please turn over for details of how to enter ⇨ F8C

HOW TO ENTER

Simply study the two pictures overleaf. They may at first glance appear the same but look closely and you should start to see the differences. There are ten to find in total, so circle them as you go on the second picture. Finally, fill in the coupon below and pop this page into an envelope and post it today. Don't forget you could win a year's supply of Mills & Boon® books—you don't even need to pay for a stamp!

Mills & Boon Spot the Difference Competition
FREEPOST CN81, Croydon, Surrey, CR9 3WZ
EIRE readers: (please affix stamp) PO Box 4546, Dublin 24.

Please tick the series you would like to receive if you are one of the lucky winners

Presents™ ❏   Enchanted™ ❏   Medical Romance™ ❏
Historical Romance™ ❏   Temptation® ❏

Are you a Reader Service™ subscriber?   Yes ❏   No ❏

Ms/Mrs/Miss/Mr ....Initials .... (BLOCK CAPITALS PLEASE)

Surname...

Address ....

....

....Postcode...........................

(I am over 18 years of age)   F8C

Closing date for entries is 31st December 1998.
One application per household. Competition open to residents of the UK and Ireland only. You may be mailed with offers from other reputable companies as a result of this application. If you would prefer not to receive such offers, please tick this box. ❏

Mills & Boon is a registered trademark owned by Harlequin Mills & Boon Limited.

COLLECTOR'S EDITION

The *Penny Jordan Collector's Edition* is
a selection of her most popular stories,
published in beautifully designed volumes
for you to collect and cherish.

*Available from Tesco, Asda, WH Smith, John Menzies,
Martins and all good paperback stockists, at £3.10 each -
or the special price of £2.80 if you use the coupon below.
On sale from 1st June 1998.*

Valid only in the UK & Eire against purchases made in retail outlets and not in
conjunction with any Reader Service or other offer.

30ᵖ OFF
COUPON
VALID UNTIL: 31.8.1998
PENNY JORDAN COLLECTOR'S EDITION

To the Customer: This coupon can be used in part payment for a
copy of PENNY JORDAN COLLECTOR'S EDITION. Only one
coupon can be used against each copy purchased. Valid only in the
UK & Eire against purchases made in retail outlets and not in
conjunction with any Reader Service or other offer. Please do not
attempt to redeem this coupon against any other product as refusal
to accept may cause embarrassment and delay at the checkout.

To the Retailer: Harlequin Mills & Boon will redeem this coupon at
face value provided only that it has been taken in part payment for
any book in the PENNY JORDAN COLLECTOR'S EDITION. The
company reserves the right to refuse payment against misredeemed
coupons. Please submit coupons to: Harlequin Mills & Boon Ltd.
NCH Dept 730, Corby, Northants NN17 1NN.

9 904170 250306 >

0472 01316